SOULMATE SYMPHONY

TAMMY SUBIA

Cover design by Ana Grigoriu-Voicu at books-design.com
ISBN 979-8-9919364-2-2

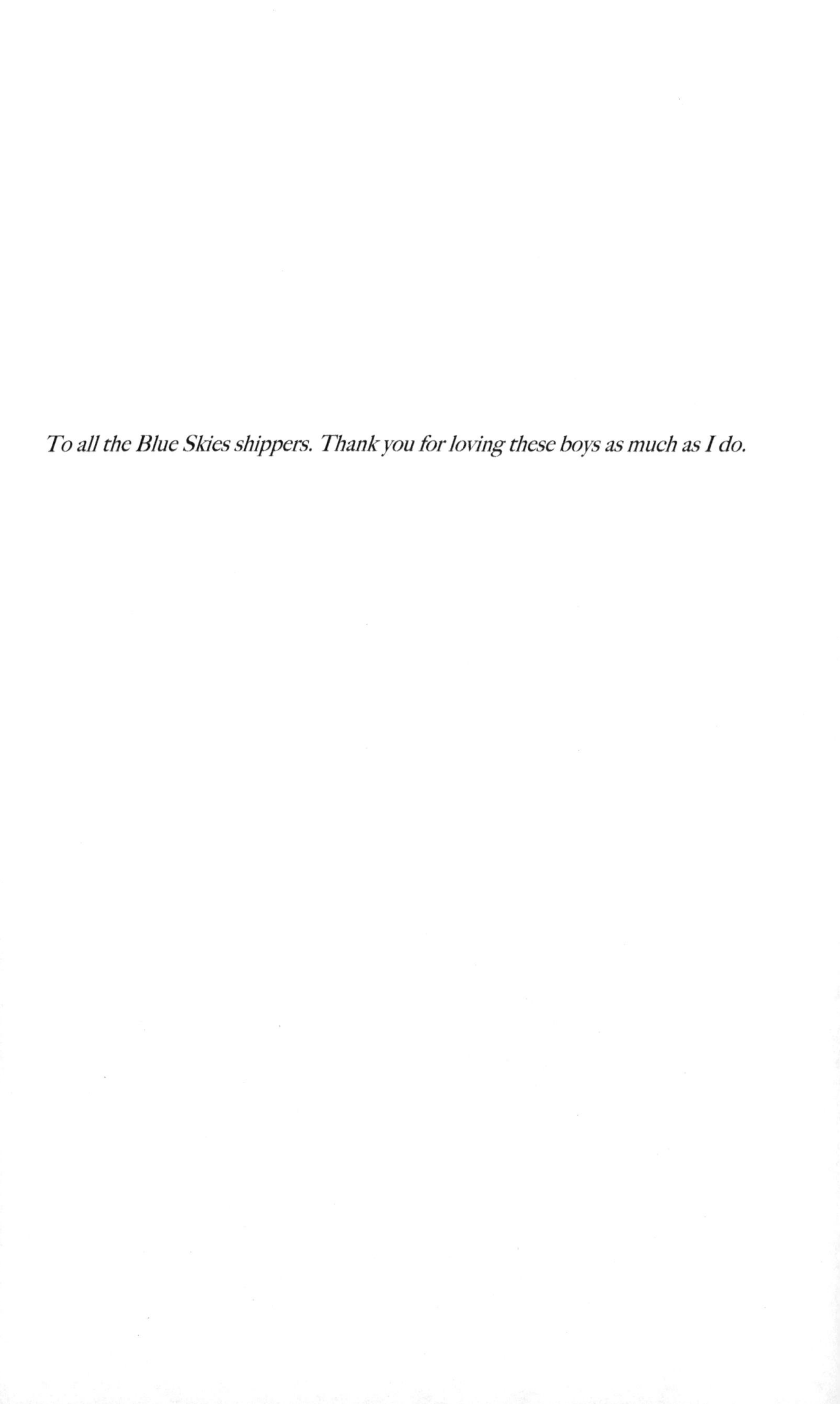

To all the Blue Skies shippers. Thank you for loving these boys as much as I do.

"SOULMATE SYMPHONY"

Song by Skyler James

Spent so much lonely time on my knees
Begging please, someone please,
Would you bring my love back to me?

Now like a miracle, here you are
The brightest sun to my stars
I've found the other half of my heart

Because you and me, we're a beautiful symphony
Lovestruck serenades, your heart sings to me
And it's all I want to hear for the rest of my life
The sounds of our sweet soulmate symphony

For years, I tried to pretend, and I ran myself thin
Ran circles, ran ragged, ran scared
But now I've run back to your arms where I'm home

We showed it off, we made such a pretty scene
Made waves, made headlines, made change
Fighting for this love we make every day

And honey, you know I'd do it all over again for you

Because you and me, we're a beautiful symphony
Lovestruck serenades, your heart sings to me
And it's all I want to hear for the rest of my life
The sounds of our sweet soulmate symphony

APRIL

SKYLER JAMES HEADLINES COACHELLA, WITH HUSBAND AND FORMER BANDMATES CHEERING HIM ON

TREVOR

THE CROWD LOSES THEIR MINDS the moment Skyler comes onstage. And they continue yelling so loudly through his first two songs that Trevor—standing in a roped off area by stage left—can barely hear him sing. Not that he needs to. He knows all of Skyler's songs by heart. But still, he'd like to enjoy his husband's smooth, honeyed voice.

At least Trevor's in the perfect spot to see him. Because *damn*, Skyler is a sight to see. He always has been. Here tonight, though, in his element, now that he's completely free to show the world who he truly is . . . he's magnificent.

He's wearing a pair of shiny purple bellbottoms that flare out extra widely on the ends. The satin material hugs his ass like a glove, making obvious every muscle he's earned from his daily yoga routines. On top, he's got only an open silver vest, showing off his chest, his perfectly defined abs, and all those tattoos.

Across his sternum, he's painted a glittery half-rainbow. Just in case there's somebody left on the planet who hasn't heard that Skyler James is very, very gay.

Trevor's happy for him and so proud. But he's also fighting his mile-long possessive streak, which is urging him to march up on that stage and throw a blanket over his man to cover him up. He'd never do that, though.

Skyler deserves to show himself off if that's what he wants to do, and the world should get to appreciate Skyler in all his glory. As long as the world knows that Trevor is the *only* one allowed to touch every inch of that glorious skin.

"I think you're drooling, bro!"

Broken out of his Skyler-induced daze, Trevor turns his head to find Oli grinning wildly at him. He leans in closer to his friend and asks, "When did you get here?"

Ten minutes before Skyler went on, Oli and Megan ran off looking for a better cell signal and enough quiet to check in with their babysitter. As excited as they were for their first big outing since becoming parents, they're having a hard time being away from Emma. But Trevor doesn't blame them. That little girl is cute as shit.

"During the first song," Oli tells him, shouting to be heard. "You were too busy being enthralled by Skyler to notice. Glad to see marriage hasn't made you two any less obsessed with each other."

No, it certainly hasn't.

As Trevor turns back to watch Skyler's performance, his mind flashes through everything that's happened since he came out publicly—both as queer and as being married to Skyler. Some of it has been a circus, but he hasn't regretted the decision. Not for a single day.

And he'd better not. Not after how damn long it took him to get there.

He should have done it sooner.

For so many years, he let all those negative voices in his head tell him how he should live his life. Voices of label executives, management, gossip reporters, talk show hosts, even random assholes in the comments sections hiding behind the anonymity of their faceless profiles.

All that time, the only voice he should have listened to was his own.

If he had done that, things would have gone differently. He and Skyler wouldn't have argued so much, wouldn't have unintentionally hurt each other. They wouldn't have imploded the way they did.

Those are wasted years he could have spent simply being happy with Skyler. It hurts that he can't get them back. But what he *can* do is ensure that he and Skyler make the most of every moment they have together from here on out. For the rest of their lives.

Although their lives will always be at least somewhat chaotic, won't they?

Because they can't erase their past fame, and Skyler's current fame is only growing larger by the day. And on top of that, Trevor's now thrown himself back into the industry with launching his new record label. It doesn't put him under the spotlight in quite the same way as when he was an artist, but because of who he is, he can never be merely a faceless exec. The ravenous media will always be there to provide commentary on what he's doing, whether he succeeds or fails.

So he'd much rather succeed.

Getting the label off the ground has been a huge undertaking, but Trevor loves the work he's doing. All the time he spends at the office, though, is time he's not spending with Skyler, which he doesn't love so much. And Skyler's obviously got a busy schedule of his own keeping him away from home, even with his tour finished. But their relationship will always be a priority.

Trevor can't say it's a hardship taking time off to come watch his husband headline Coachella.

Skyler's been playing huge venues all over the world for years, both with Boys Will Be Boys and solo, but this is his first time performing at the festival. It seems that—despite all the "concerns" their old management had—Skyler coming out as gay has actually boosted his career, if that was even possible. It's led to so many people viewing him as an even cooler artist. His boy band roots seem all but forgotten to everyone except the band's hardcore fans. And right now, he's certainly proving to any remaining critics exactly how cool he is.

Looking around at the crowd past the VIP section, Trevor can tell that everyone is having a great time. He knows not to judge anyone based on appearance, but even the people who don't look like they'd necessarily be fans of Skyler's music are grinning and dancing like this is the best moment of their lives.

That's the Skyler James effect.

The insane screaming has finally calmed down enough so that Trevor can actually hear Skyler now, though the crowd is still loudly singing along. Trevor can't help but sing along too. He's vaguely aware of the cell phones occasionally pointing his way, recording him instead of Skyler. But he's used to it by now.

He doesn't always watch Skyler's shows from such a visible spot. Sometimes he's up in a private box, or sometimes he simply watches from the side of the stage where no one can see him. It just depends on the venue, the circumstances, his mood.

The first day Trevor walked out onto that stage with Skyler and declared Skyler his husband, he made the decision to stop hiding.

When he watches Skyler's shows from a spot on the floor like this, totally out in the open, he knows it's inevitable that people will notice him, and a lot will make a big deal about it. Since he joined Skyler for his entire last tour, though, it seems the novelty of spotting him has at least somewhat worn off.

But this time, he's not the only one people are excited to see.

Oli, Noah, and Jermaine are here with him to support Skyler too. And seeing all of them together in public like this is extremely rare, so the Boys Will Be Boys fans are clearly eating it up.

Their little roped-off area needed extra security today. They've got three of the festival's staff with them, plus Skyler wanted Mike to stay with Trevor, and Jermaine's got one of his own security guys with him too.

Trevor didn't mind signing some autographs for the people who could get close enough before Skyler went on, but now he's glad he can enjoy the show without worrying about getting mobbed.

During the short transition between "The Sun and Everything" and "Soft Sunday Daydreams," however, he glances behind him and notices that Noah isn't focused on the show. He's frowning as he furiously types away on his phone.

Stepping backward, Trevor nudges him. "Hey. No work stuff. We're supposed to be having fun."

When Noah looks up, he glances around with a curious expression—as if he didn't realize he was standing in the middle of a giant, loud music festival—before his eyes land back on Trevor. "I am having fun. I just need to answer these emails."

"No, you don't. They can wait 'til Monday."

Noah looks like he's going to argue, and Trevor's prepared to use the "technically, I'm your boss" card. But then Noah sighs and slides his phone into his pocket. "There's always work to do," he says a bit begrudgingly.

If Trevor had to guess, he would say Noah's not begrudging the fact that their job is a lot of work, but rather the fact that Trevor is keeping him from doing it. Honestly, Trevor's so grateful Noah came on board to run the label with him. He has no idea how he would have done everything himself.

If anything, lately, it seems like Noah's been working even harder and longer hours than Trevor has. It's starting to get a bit concerning, actually. He seems hyperfocused on work and doesn't really talk about anything else. Trevor knows there's a lot to get done with their new artists, and they're still searching for more, but at some point, they need to find a balance. He doesn't want Noah getting burnt out so quickly.

The crowd suddenly cheers, and Trevor and Noah both look to the stage, where Skyler is bent over at the waist, shaking his purple ass at the crowd. Of course.

Noah slaps a hand on Trevor's shoulder as Trevor laughs at his husband's antics. "Yeah, so glad I'm not missing this," he says sarcastically.

Trevor elbows him. "Shut up."

"No, really," Noah says in his ear with more sincerity. "I'm glad to have you guys back in my life. I shut you both out for so long because I couldn't get over my anger, but I love you two like brothers."

Turning to eye him suspiciously, Trevor asks, "You're not dying, are you?"

Noah laughs. "No, I just . . . I guess I've done a lot of thinking over the last year. Haven't had much else to do until I started working with you."

When the crowd cheers again, Trevor whips his head back toward the stage, not wanting to miss whatever Skyler's doing now. He reaches backward to tug Noah up beside him. "All right, I love you too, man. But we should save the heart to heart for later." At a time when they can actually hear each other without losing their voices from shouting.

Something really is off with Noah. Trevor can feel it. He just doesn't know what it is.

Noah gives him a one-armed side hug, and before Trevor can return it, Oli tackles them both from behind, yelling, "Let me in on this action!" Then he's waving Jermaine over. "Come on! You too!"

Jermaine rolls his eyes, but he does move in closer until the four of them are huddled together, singing and dancing and cheering for Skyler. They've only been able to get everyone all in the same place one other time since Trevor and Skyler's wedding, so this is nice.

As much as Trevor's enjoying being with the guys, though, most of his focus remains on his husband. Skyler was definitely born for this. Trevor already knows someone is going to take a photo of this performance tonight that will be considered iconic someday. An image that illustrates the cultural phenomenon, that perfectly captures this specific, wild moment in time.

He can imagine people telling their future grandchildren the story of how they were here tonight. How they were lucky enough to witness Skyler James in his musical prime. And he wonders if maybe someday he'll get to tell *his* grandchildren about this evening. Tell them how he stood in this open field after the sun went down, the desert breeze cooling his overheated skin, as he watched their grandfather dance on stage with a rainbow painted across his chest, entirely captivating the massive crowd.

He'll tell them how he watched Skyler and thought about how damn lucky he is to have the privilege of loving and being loved by this incredible man. To experience life by his side.

During "Soulmate Symphony," the final song, Skyler struts along the stage, coming closer to where Trevor and the rest of the guys are standing. When they make eye contact, Trevor mouths *I love you*, and Skyler blows him a very exaggerated kiss.

The crowd absolutely loses it again.

Trevor can sense all the heads whipping his way to confirm who the kiss was blown to, and all he can do is grin like a lovesick fool, not taking his eyes off Skyler.

Because yeah. That's his fucking baby up there.

SKYLER

WHAT A FUCKING RUSH.

As a security team escorts Skyler off the stage and to his trailer, he's still basking in the adrenaline high from his performance. This feeling will never get old. Once the adrenaline wears off, he's going to realize how exhausted he is, and he'll probably crash hard. But right now it feels like he could do another whole set.

The security team doesn't leave him until he's opened the trailer door, and as soon as he steps inside, he trades being surrounded by one group of men for being surrounded by another. Not that he's complaining.

Oli is the first to rush him, throwing his arms around Skyler's neck in a hug. On instinct, Skyler's arms start to wind around Oli's waist to hug him back, but Oli quickly pulls away, making a face. "Ew, you're all sweaty."

Skyler scoffs. "What do you expect when I just performed in the desert?"

"You went on at night only half-dressed," Oli argues.

"Under all those stage lights, dancing and running around. Don't act like you don't know how it goes."

Despite his rightful defense of himself, Skyler lifts an arm to smell his pit, then wrinkles his nose. Yeah, he could definitely use a shower. He only wishes he could do it in his own home, with his luxurious rainfall showerhead, rather than in the trailer's cramped stall with the dubious water pressure. And he also wants to spend some time with the guys before he's ready to pass out, so the shower can wait a bit.

When Oli moves back, Jermaine steps up and slings an arm around Skyler's shoulder, pulling Skyler briefly into his side. "Good job, man. You rocked that."

"Thanks," Skyler says, beaming at him.

Noah gives him a hearty slap on the back and offers his own praise. And when Skyler spots Megan sitting at the table, she smiles and congratulates him. Then the guys back off enough for him to see Trevor, who's sitting casually on the couch, legs splayed slightly open, and Skyler all but forgets anyone else is here.

He beelines past Mike on his way to his husband, and when he reaches him, he doesn't hesitate to lower himself onto Trevor's lap, straddling him. Trevor's hands come up to grip his waist, and the smile he's giving Skyler is full of admiration, sunshine, and love, love, love.

"Did you like it?" Skyler asks.

"Of course, I did." Trevor slides his palm up Skyler's ribcage, and Skyler suddenly remembers how sweaty he is, but he's not about to move out of Trevor's grasp just yet. "You were incredible, baby. You always are."

Unable to control himself, Skyler dives down for a kiss, and Trevor doesn't hesitate in returning it with equal enthusiasm.

It only takes a few seconds for Oli to shout out, "Oh no! Can't you guys wait 'til you're alone?"

Someone else—Noah, he thinks, but maybe it's Mike—mutters an agreement.

Trevor doesn't break the kiss, but Skyler feels his arm moving behind Skyler's back. More than likely, he's flipping everyone off. Skyler doesn't want to be rude, though, so he only indulges himself in a few more moments of his husband's lips before he pulls away and hops off Trevor's lap.

"Who wants a drink?" he asks.

Jermaine holds up his beer. "We already started without you."

"That's cool. I want a drink, then."

Trevor stands, taking Skyler's hand and crossing with him to the small fridge. "I didn't let them have your spiked iced teas," he says. Then, frowning, he adds, "Well, actually, I gave Megan one, but I kept Oli away from them."

"Which was very mean, by the way," Oli complains.

Skyler kisses Trevor on the cheek and grabs himself a can. When he follows Trevor back to sit on the couch, he leaves at least some semblance of space between them, still aware of his sweaty state and possible odor. But Trevor reaches out and drags him closer, wrapping an arm around Skyler and urging him to lean against him.

"Even though I'm sweaty?" Skyler questions, though he can't resist snuggling closer.

"Yeah, baby," Trevor says. "I don't mind."

Grinning, Skyler teases him. "*Ooh*, you really *looove* me."

But Trevor's response doesn't sound anything like a joke when he says, "Damn right, I do."

Skyler's heart does a quick little tap dance in his chest. It's wild how Trevor can still do that to him, even after all these years.

"Oh boy, here they go again," Oli groans as Skyler leans in for a kiss.

Skyler pouts, hesitating. He wasn't going to make out with him. He just wanted a kiss. And he's allowed to kiss his husband whenever he wants, okay? After spending five lonely years without Trevor—deprived of the best kisses and cuddles—Skyler refuses to hold himself back anymore. Especially when they're in a safe space like this.

It's clear Trevor feels the same, because he cradles the back of Skyler's head and pulls him all the way in until their lips meet. Yeah, they're the annoying PDA couple now. But these guys should be used to this anyway.

As they exchange a few chaste kisses, Oli says, "Okay, I love you guys, and I love that you're in love, but I'm starting to feel like chopped liver over here."

"I'll kiss you later, hon," Megan says.

Someone laughs, but Oli continues to whine something about "gross lovebirds being gross."

Skyler knows Oli's only teasing them. Oli can never miss an opportunity to open his mouth and give someone shit. It doesn't bother Skyler in the slightest, but he still appreciates it when he hears Noah say, "Leave them alone."

That's new.

Even though he and Noah made up, and Noah's forgiven Skyler for his past fuckups, the relationship between the two of them hasn't quite gotten back to the way it was before all the drama. And that's fine. They can be friends without being super close. Skyler was always closer with Jermaine anyway.

But he's glad Noah and Trevor have fully rebuilt their friendship. He's glad Trevor has Noah to share the stress of running his label with. They always worked well together in the past. That is, when they weren't at each other's throats over something that had to do with Trevor and Skyler's relationship, of course.

Anyway, back in the band days, Noah was usually the one making comments about the two of them. So it's cool that he's defending them now.

Having gotten his temporary fill of Trevor's kisses—because he'll never *really* get his fill, even if he kisses him a hundred times a day for the rest of his life—Skyler rests his head on Trevor's shoulder and gives his attention to the group.

They all chat while everyone but Mike has a couple drinks. Jermaine's the only one not living in L.A., so Skyler's really happy to spend some time with him and hear about the new sneaker line Jermaine designed and is getting ready to launch. But it's not long before Skyler starts to fade. The drive back to Malibu will take a few hours, so they were planning to leave in the morning, but suddenly, all Skyler wants is to get home to his shower and his own bed.

"What's wrong, baby?" Trevor asks quietly, gently turning Skyler's chin toward him. "You look ready to drop. Want me to kick everyone out?"

He shakes his head. "I don't wanna sleep here. I wanna go home."

"We can do that. Whatever you want," Trevor assures him. Then he yells out to Mike, who is half-slumped over the table, scrolling on his phone. "Hey, Mike, do you think you'd be able to stay awake long enough to drive us home if we leave now?"

Sitting up straighter, Mike nods. "Find me a very large cup of coffee and I'll be good."

"Wait, no!" Oli protests. "We're supposed to be partying. You can't just cut off the fun."

"Ignore him," Megan says with an eye roll. "He can't stop worrying about Emma anyway. We should get home too."

"You guys can all stay here if you want," Skyler offers. "I'm just exhausted, I'm sorry."

Noah gets up, stretching his arms above his head. "No need to apologize."

With that settled, they all say their goodbyes and get ready to head out.

Skyler changes into sweatpants and a hoodie to be more comfortable, then Mike leads him and Trevor to the Escalade. In the backseat, he angles himself sideways and leans against the window. When Trevor pulls Skyler's legs over his lap, Skyler is sure he'll be asleep within minutes.

"Love you," he murmurs, closing his eyes as Trevor starts massaging his calves.

That's the last thing he remembers until Trevor is cradling his face and gently coaxing him awake.

With an arm around Skyler's waist, Trevor lets Skyler lean his weight sleepily against him as they go in the house and up to their bedroom. *Very nice. Ten out of ten service.*

Skyler heads right for the bed, but Trevor grabs him before he can get there, steering him into the ensuite bathroom instead. "Shower, remember?"

Shaking his head, Skyler whines, "*Nooo*, too tired. Just wanna sleep."

"Come on. You know you'll feel better if you go to bed clean," Trevor tells him. Rather than push him into the shower, though, Trevor leads him over to their obscenely large, jacuzzi-style tub and sits him on the edge. "Don't fall over."

Skyler sticks his tongue out at him, because it feels like the right thing to do. And maybe because he gets childish when he's exhausted. But then he realizes Trevor is filling the tub for him and pouring in his lavender bath salts, and suddenly, a bath sounds like the best idea in the world.

When the tub is full, Trevor helps Skyler get undressed and into it before quickly stripping down and climbing in behind him, urging Skyler to lean back against his chest. For a few minutes, he simply holds him like this, fingers tracing idly over Skyler's skin.

Skyler's so nice and relaxed that he could pass out again, but he twists his head to give Trevor a kiss instead. Then Trevor grabs the body wash and bath sponge he left on the edge of the tub and begins washing Skyler gently. Skyler practically purrs like a cat under the treatment. This is even better than the rainfall showerhead.

Trevor carefully washes his hair for him too. When he's done, he trails kisses down Skyler's neck and along the top of his shoulder. Skyler squirms happily, unintentionally pressing his ass farther into Trevor's lap. Or possibly not so unintentionally.

"No sex," Trevor tells him. "You need to get some more sleep."

Despite agreeing with him, Skyler sighs as dramatically as he can manage when he's this tired. "You're a mean daddy."

Trevor pinches his side, causing him to jolt and splash a bit of water out of the tub. "Don't make me spank you."

"That's not supposed to be a threat, is it?" Skyler mumbles around a long yawn. And Trevor just laughs softly, holding him a little tighter.

They don't stay in the bath much longer, because Skyler's really struggling to keep his eyes open. After helping him get out, Trevor wraps Skyler in a fluffy towel to dry him off, then leads him to bed. And as soon as they're both under the covers, Trevor reaches for Skyler to draw him closer.

Snuggling up against his husband, Skyler lets a gentle wave of contentment wash over him, lulling him to a peaceful sleep.

His life is so good.

Everything he's gone through in the past—the stress, cruel management, self-destruction, professional and personal breakups—somehow, it was all worth it. His past made him who he is today, and he's earned all the incredible things he has now. His career, this house, this unbelievably wonderful man sharing his bed.

Maybe some things could've been easier for him, but it doesn't matter anymore. He wouldn't trade being married to Trevor for anything.

MAY

TREVOR BLUE SIGNS NEW ARTIST TO SUN & STAR RECORDS

TREVOR

TREVOR WAKES UP BEFORE HIS ALARM and immediately notes the absence of Skyler's body wrapped around his. He blindly reaches an arm out, patting the mattress in search of him. Giving up, he opens his eyes and is disappointed to find that Skyler is nowhere in their bed. His phone tells him he still has some time before he needs to get up and ready for work. Not a ton of time, but certainly enough for a good cuddle—or potentially more—if only his husband were here.

Skyler doesn't have anywhere to be this morning, but he's an early riser. More than likely, he's downstairs doing yoga.

Right as Trevor thinks this, the bedroom door opens and Skyler strolls in looking a bit flushed. He's wearing a loose white tank with a tiny pair of orange shorts, his hair up in a bun. At noticing that Trevor's awake, he smiles and says, "Morning, babe," then comes around to Trevor's side of the bed, leaning down to give him a quick kiss. Too quick for Trevor's liking.

He tries to urge Skyler down on top of him, intent on kissing him some more, but Skyler moves away too fast. Trevor lets out a noise of protest and resorts to making grabby hands to get him to come back, a behavior he picked up from his husband.

Skyler laughs. "I'm gonna hop in the shower."

"Okay," Trevor relents. "But go really fast, then get back in bed with me."

It takes Skyler a second to catch the hungry way Trevor is eyeing him, and then he grins. "Got it. Fastest shower ever."

Trevor smiles to himself as he watches Skyler scurry into the bathroom. It would be more efficient if he went to shower with him, but he's too lazy to get out of bed yet. And this morning, he'd rather fool around on their Egyptian cotton sheets than in the shower. So he reaches into his boxers, idly stroking himself while he waits.

True to his word, it only takes Skyler minutes. He obviously skipped washing his hair, which is still in the bun, and he's naked, which is perfect.

"C'mere," Trevor says fondly, holding an arm out in invitation.

Skyler promptly obliges, crawling onto the bed and straddling Trevor's thighs. Trevor grabs one of his hips and uses his other hand around the back of Skyler's neck to drag Skyler's mouth down to his. Skyler's lips taste sweet, and even though Trevor has kissed this man a million times, he'll never get over the taste of him. Or the way Trevor's heart starts to sing for him as they exchange slow, languid kisses. He captures Skyler's bottom lip gently with his teeth, pulling it into his mouth to suck on it, and Skyler lets out a tiny sound of approval.

They kiss like they're pouring their love into each other. Like they're in no hurry, because in this bed together is the only place they need to be.

But sadly, Trevor does need to speed this up if he wants to make Skyler come before he has to get going. So he flips their positions, getting Skyler on his back and nudging Skyler's thighs apart to make room for himself in between them. He kisses his way down Skyler's neck, chest, and abs, tracing his tongue over the tattoos, until he reaches Skyler's cock. It's already hard and straining toward him.

When he ignores it and moves to suck gently on the sensitive skin of Skyler's inner thigh instead, Skyler whines.

"Shh, baby," Trevor soothes. "I've got you. Can you grab the lube for me?"

Skyler rolls over to reach into their bedside drawer, then tosses the bottle onto the mattress. Trevor takes it and squeezes a bit onto his fingers, rubbing them with his thumb to warm it. Instinctually, Skyler bends his knees to give Trevor better access to his hole, and Trevor begins running his index finger in slow circles around Skyler's rim.

"*Mmm*," Skyler moans softly.

Trevor teases him some more before pushing the tip of his index finger inside.

"More," Skyler demands immediately.

That makes Trevor chuckle. "Greedy boy."

But he always gives this man what he wants, so he slides his finger the rest of the way into Skyler's tight body. It doesn't take much time at all for Skyler to loosen up for him, allowing Trevor to add a second finger. He gently scissors them apart to loosen Skyler up some more before giving him a third.

Now Skyler's letting out a steady stream of moans as Trevor fucks in and out of him at a languid pace.

Trevor curls his fingers and brushes against Skyler's prostate, watching in amusement as Skyler's hips jolt off the bed in response. "You like that, baby?"

"Mmhmm," Skyler murmurs, sounding lust-drunk. It usually takes him much longer to reach this almost delirious state, but maybe the ease and laziness of the early morning hour have factored in here, helping him relax fully.

Shuffling a little farther down the bed, Trevor bends down to lick around Skyler's rim as he continues to finger him. Skyler's thighs start to tremble beside Trevor's head, and god, Trevor will never get tired of this. He'll never stop wanting his beautiful, sexy husband.

"You want another finger?" he asks.

The noise Skyler makes could be interpreted either way, but when Trevor glances up, he finds Skyler nodding his head frantically against the pillow, mussing up his hair. So he reaches for more lube, then slowly eases his pinky into Skyler's hole alongside the other three fingers.

He picks up his finger-fucking pace, but not by much. He can tell Skyler wants it faster, harder, but Trevor's enjoying this too much to rush it. Ducking his head down, he licks at Skyler's rim some more, managing to fit the tip of his tongue into Skyler's already stuffed hole.

Then he moves his mouth up, sucking a bit at the skin of Skyler's taint until he reaches his balls. Skyler moans obscenely when Trevor sucks one into his mouth. After he gives the other the same treatment, Trevor moves up farther until he can get his mouth around the head of Skyler's leaking cock. Even Skyler's precum tastes sweet. Trevor hums in approval, chasing the taste with his tongue.

Skyler thrusts his hips upward, trying to force himself deeper into Trevor's mouth, but Trevor's not having it.

"Not yet, baby. Let me play with you some more."

"So close," is all Skyler responds.

"I know you are. Know your body so well, don't I? Don't I always take good care of you?"

"Yes, yes, yes!" Skyler chants. Though whether that's in answer to Trevor's question, or in encouragement of the way Trevor is now pressing against his prostate, it's hard to say.

Either way, Trevor continues to torture him, softly licking at his cock while using his fingers to bring him right to the edge before backing off. But he can sense Skyler's growing frustration and knows he's nearly reaching his limit.

As Trevor's about to start sucking Skyler for real, his alarm goes off, startling him. Surely, Skyler must hear the sound too, but he doesn't seem to care. He just keeps whining and moaning and writhing on Trevor's hand.

Unable to resist messing with him, Trevor carefully pulls his fingers out of Skyler's hole, then gets off the bed. "All right, well, I should get ready for work."

Skyler sits up so fast he probably made himself dizzy. "You better not leave me like this!" he says, sounding panicked.

"Sorry, baby, gotta go," Trevor teases.

"You're the boss of the whole damn company! You can be five minutes late!"

Trevor pretends to consider it for a second before he smirks. "Anything for you, baby."

This time, when he crawls back on the bed and in between Skyler's legs, he wastes no more time in taking Skyler's cock down his throat. He slides two fingers back into Skyler's hole as he sucks him off in earnest now. And in less than a minute, Skyler's release is filling his mouth.

As his orgasm subsides, Skyler goes boneless, sinking farther into the mattress. He murmurs something that sounds like approval or appreciation.

Trevor gives him one final kiss on the inside of his thigh, then pats his leg lightly before he gets up again. Now he really does need to hustle. He gets ready quickly, leaving Skyler sated and dozing in bed.

Skyler stirs, though, as Trevor approaches the side of the bed, dressed in a powder blue button-up and fitted gray slacks. "You're leaving?" he asks quietly, still sounding a bit hazy.

"You knew I had to go to work," Trevor reminds him gently.

"Doesn't mean I want you to," Skyler says, rolling onto his side to give Trevor puppy dog eyes. "You should stay here and cuddle me all day."

"That sounds perfect, baby, but I can't."

It does kind of suck. The way that Skyler's schedule has been a bit more relaxed now that he finished his tour, while at the same time, Trevor has launched the label, so his schedule has filled up. He wishes he could spend every day doing nothing more than being with Skyler. And honestly, he could. They could do that if they both decided to stop working. But neither of them wants that.

Trevor spent years doing pretty much nothing, and it wasn't good for him. He's happy to have found his purpose—other than loving Skyler, of course—and to be working again at something he feels good about.

Someday they'll retire. Maybe buy a private island and move there, away from the rest of the world. Just the two of them.

Except he knows they'd miss their friends and Skyer's family—*their* family.

"We'll make sure we take a whole day off together this week," he promises. Then he thinks about all the meetings he has lined up and amends it to, "Or next week."

Skyler frowns again, but then he beckons Trevor closer, and when Trevor leans down, Skyler smiles and kisses him sweetly. "Go be a big shot. I might try to work on some new songs if I feel inspired, and I'll prep us dinner for when you get home."

"I love you," Trevor tells him.

"I love you more," Skyler says.

Trevor shakes his head. "Not possible."

He gives Skyler one more kiss before heading out. They'll never agree on that, but he knows in his heart he's right. Because he's certain he loves Skyler more than another person has ever loved anyone else in the history of the world.

THE RECORD LABEL'S OFFICES and recording studio are housed in a large building in downtown L.A., so Trevor dealt with some annoying traffic on his commute. Still, he greets the lobby receptionist with a wide smile and little wave as he strolls past her desk and into the elevator. He makes his way up to the top floor, then to the end of the long hallway. Like always, his eyes flit to the plaque on the wall that says SUN & STAR RECORDS, and he feels a dash of pride before opening the door.

They have three offices and a conference room up here, with their studio down on the second floor. That's all they need for now. The third office doesn't get any use, but it's good to have it for whenever they might need to hire another executive.

Trevor is about to turn toward his office when Noah pops so quickly out of his own on the opposite side of the hall that they nearly crash into each other. "Jesus," Trevor mutters, trying to veer around him. But Noah won't get out of his way.

"You're late," Noah says sharply.

"Only a few minutes."

Completely blocking Trevor's doorway now, Noah awkwardly crosses his arms over his chest whiles holding a takeout coffee cup in one hand. His scowl feels completely unnecessary. "It looks bad for you to be late."

Trevor eyes him critically and asks, "What's gotten up your ass?"

"Nothing." Noah thrusts the cup out at Trevor. "I stopped and got you a double espresso from that place around the corner you like. It's your fault if it's cold."

"Thanks," Trevor says, accepting the beverage and hoping Noah will move past this unexplained bad mood. "But you know you're not my assistant, right? You don't need to get me coffee."

"No shit. Can't I just get you coffee as your friend?"

Choosing not to comment again on the attitude, Trevor thanks him once more and juts his head toward his office. Noah takes the hint and steps aside, allowing Trevor to go in. But to Trevor's growing annoyance, Noah follows right behind him. Trevor rounds his desk and sinks into his stupidly expensive chair. His ass doesn't even get a second to enjoy it, though, because Noah is hovering over the other side of the desk, still looking disappointed or disgruntled or whatever the hell he is.

"What?" Trevor asks warily.

"Jasper Bell is in the conference room."

"Now?" Trevor frowns. "Our meeting isn't until . . ."

"He got here thirty minutes early," Noah fills in for him. "Unlike some people."

"Okay, can you chill?" Trevor finally snaps. Because seriously. Noah's always been wound a little tightly, but lately it seems to be getting worse.

Noah winces. "Yeah. Sorry. I just wanna make sure things go smoothly here, and that we don't make any mistakes."

Trevor glances at the framed photo on his desk. He hasn't done much decorating in here, but the photo of him and Skyler on their wedding day was the first thing he put out. Looking at Skyler on the happiest day of their lives helps him find some patience before he returns his focus to Noah.

"I appreciate that," he tells him. "I really do. But things are going great so far. Better than we could've expected, honestly. You need to relax, man."

With a self-deprecating smile, Noah says, "We all know I'm not the best at that."

Definitely true. And that's why Trevor's concerned. Because Noah took too much responsibility on his shoulders years ago when it came to the band. Tried to control stuff he had no way of controlling. Trevor saw what that did to him, and he doesn't want it to happen again.

"I promise if there's any kind of problem, I'll let you know," he assures his friend.

"Okay." Noah's demeanor visibly shifts into professional mode, but his next words dampen the effect. "Let's not keep your little protégé waiting any longer."

Trevor sighs, grabbing his coffee as he stands. Noah's right about not keeping Jasper waiting, but—"I wish you'd stop calling him that."

"I could call him Goth Skyler instead."

"Stop."

Giving a short nod, Noah says, "I'll try." Then he spins and heads briskly out of Trevor's office, urging Trevor with a, "Now come on," over his shoulder.

Trevor can't figure out why Noah doesn't like the new artist Trevor signed. It's clear to Trevor that the guy is immensely talented. And he loves how Jasper is totally open about his sexuality. He made it clear in his first meeting with Trevor that he wasn't willing to hide who he is in order to get a record deal.

Trevor assured him that he was interested in the whole package. That who Jasper is as a person is as equally important to Trevor as who he is as an artist. Because he's tired of the entertainment industry pushing shitty people to the top and then expecting the audience to separate the art from the artist. And, of course, he's really fucking tired of crusty old executives acting like an artist being openly queer would be detrimental to their career.

Fuck that.

He swore to himself he would do things differently with his own label.

As Trevor opens the door to the conference room, he catches Jasper practically launching himself out of his chair to stand before Trevor even takes a step inside. "Hello," Trevor says, pretending that wasn't a little awkward.

Jasper looks nervous. "Hi. Sorry I was so early."

"That's not something to apologize for," Trevor tells him with a shake of his head. "I was running a bit late."

It's hard not to smile at the memory of *why* he was late, but he manages. He gestures for Jasper to sit back down, then takes his own seat at the head of the unnecessarily long table. Noah sits opposite Jasper, and after the required pleasantries, they get down to business.

Jasper shares ideas he had for changes on a few of his songs. He plays them clips he recorded on his phone and articulates why he thinks the changes work better.

One thing Trevor's noticed about Jasper is how he manages to come off as totally confident in some situations, while seeming entirely unsure of himself in others. It's strange. Trevor can tell that Jasper is confident in his music—as he should be. But it almost feels like he's so grateful to be given this opportunity that he's afraid of making a misstep or pushing too hard for something.

It reminds Trevor of the way he and the other guys were when the band was formed. And though he would never manipulate or take advantage of his artists the way their label did to them, he wants to make sure Jasper understands that he can and *should* always advocate for himself the way he did in his first meeting with Trevor.

After they go over Jasper's ideas, and Trevor gives him the green light to make the changes, the three of them head downstairs to the recording studio to start laying down some vocals.

While Jasper gets set up in the booth, Trevor and Noah settle in on the other side of the glass. Trevor watches Jasper remove his leather jacket, revealing a full tattooed sleeve on one arm and a line of leather and beaded bracelets going up the other. A silver chain hangs from one hip over his dark gray jeans, which are cuffed over a pair of black combat boots. His black, shaggy hair curls around his face. It nearly obscures his eyes, but from seeing him up close in the conference room, Trevor's pretty sure he's wearing eyeliner.

Okay, so maybe Trevor can see why Noah would call him "Goth Skyler."

"Let's start with 'Mind Over Matter,'" Trevor says once Jasper is perched on the edge of a stool, the headphones around his neck and a water bottle on the table beside him.

He sounds great on the first verse, but then in the chorus, his voice cracks on a high note. Immediately, he tries again, and although he doesn't crack this time, it still doesn't sound right. Before Trevor can tell him that, Jasper grimaces and says, "Sorry. I can do it, just gimme a sec."

Trevor reaches forward, pressing the button on the switchboard that allows him to talk back. "No worries, take your time."

Noah shakes his head as Trevor leans back in his chair again. "I just don't see what the big deal is with this kid. He's not that great."

"He's not a kid," Trevor reminds him.

"He's twenty-four. Close enough."

"He's only six years younger than you, and plenty older than all of us were when we joined the band."

Noah frowns, looking contemplative for a moment. Then he says, "And look how well that turned out for us."

Trevor sighs. Even though Boys Will Be Boys was a massive success, he understands what Noah's getting at. They were too young to be thrust into near instant fame and deal with all the shit they dealt with, but that's not the point.

Jasper definitely isn't a kid, and he *is* great. He has the potential to be incredible. Trevor could see that in him right away.

This label has earned a respectable reputation faster than Trevor could have hoped. He's already signed some really talented acts. But *this*. This is what he's been waiting for. Someone like Jasper Bell to come out of nowhere and stun the world.

Jasper is authentic, he cares deeply about his music and the messages he wants to convey through his songs, and he's got everything in him to be a real star. The kind of artist people will remember decades after he stops making music.

Like Skyler.

Trevor won't say that Jasper is going to be the next Skyler James. Because Skyler is so uniquely in his own lane that it's hard to imagine anyone else comparing.

And Jasper isn't wearing sequins and waving rainbows. Instead, he sings about being queer in a way that's understated. That's quietly beautiful and sometimes heartbreaking. Simple and nuanced in the same breath.

The demo he sent was great, but the first time Trevor watched him sing in person, he knew Jasper had something special. He drew Trevor's focus right to him, to the emotions painted on his face. He's captivating, hard to look away from. He peels back his own layers with every note and makes you desperate to find out what's waiting at his core.

Honestly, it's crazy that Noah doesn't see that.

But Trevor has a feeling that whatever Noah's issue is with Jasper, it has less to do with Jasper and more to do with Noah. He's still sensing something might be going on with Noah. Something beyond the typical work stress. He has no idea what it could be, but he hopes Noah will come to him if there's anything he can do to help.

They take longer in the studio than they expected to for today, but by the end, Jasper has recorded vocals for three tracks that everyone is happy with. Even Noah begrudgingly admitted they sounded good.

After Jasper leaves, Trevor has a few phone calls to make and a new demo in his inbox to check out. He's just packing up his stuff, finally ready to head home, when he gets a text from Skyler.

Peanuts or blueberries?

What? he writes back.

For dinner.

Trevor smiles. He has no idea how peanuts could be used in a dinner, and blueberries sound like dessert, but he never underestimates Skyler's cooking skills.

Peanuts, he answers. Because Skyler's already sweet enough, and Trevor's planning on eating *him* for dessert.

JUNE

SKYLER JAMES CAST AS VOICE OF FIRST QUEER DISNEY PRINCE

SKYLER

AS SKYLER GIVES THE ASPARAGUS he's sautéing an idle toss, he uses his free hand to flip the page of the script he has open beside him on the counter. He's already practiced his lines probably more than he needs to, but he keeps doing it in every spare moment, because he's determined to get them perfect.

This role means a lot to him.

He still hasn't gotten over the surprise and elation he felt the moment his agent called and told him Disney was interested in having him audition for a voice acting role. He gave up acting as a teenager when he joined the band, and his music career has kept him so busy ever since then, that he never stopped to consider pursuing it again. But the producer said she and the writers already had Skyler in mind when they came up with the concept for the movie.

Which is flattering and awesome, but also, a smidge terrifying. Because this is a big deal. A gay Disney prince? Despite how far society has come, that's not something Skyler ever thought he'd see.

And now he's going to *be* that prince.

A whole new generation of kids will get to grow up seeing queerness more normalized. Some of them will see themselves represented in a children's movie for the first time.

Skyler can't let them down.

As soon as he found out he got the part, he started doing research on voice acting. Even though he won't be on screen, he knows his facial expressions affect the delivery of the lines, so he's fully getting into character now as he reads his lines out loud to his captive audience.

Okay. So maybe his only audience is Stella, and she's far more captivated by the food he's cooking than by him. But still.

"I wouldn't do that if I were you." He tries to inject a bit of humor and playfulness into the warning. "The queen is very particular about her teacups."

As he skims the other character's lines, the oven beeps, and he has to stop to take his pan out. Setting it on the stove, he quickly flips the sweet potato slices and sprinkles some cheese on top of the chicken before popping the pan back in the oven and resetting the timer for eight more minutes.

When he glances over at Stella, she's still waiting fairly patiently for something good to eat, so he reaches for a bag of dog treats they keep on the counter and tosses a couple to her. She catches them effortlessly in her mouth but makes no move to exit the kitchen. She's smart enough to wait for the chicken.

Going back to his script, Skyler finishes reading his lines for the short meet-cute scene, then flips a couple pages to his next one, where the prince runs into the boy again.

"Fancy seeing you here," he says cheekily, as he cocks one hip out to the side.

"I live here," comes a voice from behind him, making Skyler jump and squeal in a very undignified way.

Spinning around with a hand to his chest, he tells his husband, "Oh my god, don't do that."

Trevor chuckles. "Sorry. Couldn't resist."

Skyler makes an unimpressed face, then widens his eyes as Trevor strides across the kitchen like he's on a mission. When he reaches Skyler, he grabs him by the hips, pushing him gently against the counter. Before Skyler can offer him a proper greeting, Trevor kisses him, his tongue immediately delving into Skyler's mouth. He takes what he wants, and all Skyler can do is let him. Skyler's out of breath by the time Trevor pulls back with a hungry look still in his eyes.

And scratch that. That was the most proper of proper greetings. Who needs silly little words like *hello*?

"Did you have a good day at work, honey?" Skyler jokes in his best fifties housewife voice, though he's still a little breathless.

"Mmhmm." Trevor nods, but his gaze is focused down at Skyler's hip bones as his thumbs rub circles over them. "We're almost finished recording Jasper's album, and I'm really happy with it."

"That's great! I can't wait to hear it."

Trevor has shared bits of songs with Skyler already, sometimes asking his opinion, or sometimes just excited about them. But Skyler wants to hear the whole thing. And he hasn't met Jasper yet, but he wants to do that too. With as highly as Trevor speaks about him, Skyler's sure he's going to love him.

Stella lets out a whine and paws at Trevor's pant leg, obviously jealous that she isn't getting her own greeting. Trevor smiles at her, giving her a, "Hey, girl," as he squats down to scratch behind her ears. Her tail thumps loudly against the kitchen floor.

When he stands back up, Trevor's eyes flit to the script on the counter. "Were you practicing your lines again?"

"Yeah," Skyler tells him. "Will you read with me after dinner?"

"Of course. But you know I'm not an actor."

"That's fine. It just helps to not be talking to myself."

Trevor smiles teasingly. "Like you were doing when I walked in?"

"You weren't supposed to hear that," Skyler says, turning back to his cooking.

The asparagus is slightly charred, the way he likes it, so he moves them off the hot burner. Trevor crowds behind him, kissing and nipping gently at the junction between his neck and shoulder, and Skyler squirms in delight under the treatment. He presses his ass backward into Trevor almost involuntarily.

"Can I make up my own lines?" Trevor asks. Sliding a hand up Skyler's sternum until his fingertips graze Skyler's throat, he adopts a ridiculous voice and says, "Take me now, my fair prince."

Skyler giggles. "I'm pretty sure there's no line that says that."

"Well, there should be." With his free hand, Trevor gently tugs at the purple scrunchie holding Skyler's hair up in a messy bun, letting the hair spill down past his shoulders. "Is it going to be weird if I'm attracted to the cartoon version of you?"

Skyler makes a face, even as he tilts his head back, enjoying Trevor's fingers running over his scalp. "Um, yes. I think so."

"Okay, fine," Trevor says, the fingers of his other hand creeping farther upward until they wrap loosely around Skyler's throat. "Guess I'll just stick to lusting after the real thing."

The oven timer beeps, and Skyler whimpers when he tries to lean forward but Trevor only tightens his grip, holding him back. "Dinner's going to burn," he protests weakly.

Trevor squeezes his throat, twisting his other hand in Skyler's hair and pulling him backward a couple steps. "That's okay, because I want to eat you instead."

Even though Skyler is so totally on board with that plan, he makes another noise of protest and struggles to get away. "Wait, seriously, let me take the chicken out first."

Trevor releases him with a put-upon sigh. "If you must."

"You're the one who's gonna complain later when you're hungry."

"Don't worry. I'm sure I'll be getting my fill in just a minute."

Okay, Skyler's trying to do the responsible thing here, but he only has so much self-control. He grabs a dish towel and hastily takes the pan out of the oven, setting it on top of the stove. Now the food won't burn, but it will get cold. The way Trevor is devouring him with his eyes when Skyler turns back to him, though, has that concern quickly slipping from Skyler's mind.

When Trevor reaches for him, Skyler's ready this time and reaches out too, curling his fingers into the soft, smooth material of Trevor's work shirt. He slips his other hand into Trevor's back pocket to give his ass a squeeze. Meanwhile, Trevor has one arm wrapped around Skyler's waist, and his other hand is traveling back up teasingly close to Skyler's throat again.

Skyler moans when Trevor maneuvers one leg in between his, using his thigh to apply a slight pressure on Skyler's rapidly hardening cock.

"You like that, baby, don't you?" Trevor says huskily.

Skyler barely has a chance to nod before Trevor is grabbing his head with both hands, using his hold to tilt Skyler's face whichever way he wants as he kisses him. Like Skyler's a doll for Trevor to arrange to his liking.

Making little movements with his hips, Skyler attempts to ride Trevor's thigh. But Trevor stops him, pulling away from the kiss and gripping Skyler's waist. He steps backward, taking Skyler with him until they're at the island. That's where Trevor spins them, so Skyler feels the countertop pressed into his back again.

Trevor undresses him, doing it efficiently, rather than making a big show of it. Although he does pause his work long enough to suck a mark into Skyler's pec, right above his nipple. Once Skyler is standing there completely naked, with Trevor still fully dressed, Trevor flips him around, and Skyler finds himself bent over the island, his chest pressed to the cool marble.

He shivers, both from the feeling on his skin and from Trevor's hands skimming up and down his sides. Then Trevor leans over his back and Skyler feels a kiss pressed to the top knot of his spine. And then another one below that. And farther and farther down as Trevor makes a path toward his tailbone.

As he reaches it, Skyler is relieved, because it means his ass will finally get some attention. At this point, he's dying to have something inside him. His hard cock is jutting uncomfortably into the side of the island.

But no. Instead of moving down between his cheeks, Trevor starts making his way back up Skyler's spine, leaving another trail of kisses. In other circumstances, Skyler would love this sweet treatment, but not right now. Not after Trevor's hot display of aggression. Not after he allowed his dinner to be forgotten and let Trevor strip him down in the middle of the damn kitchen. He needs more action.

"I thought you were going to eat me," he taunts. "Stop playing with your food."

"Hush," Trevor demands, giving his ass a sharp slap that makes Skyler yelp. "I'll take my time if I want to."

Skyler turns his head to the side and attempts to glare at his husband without lifting his chest from the counter. "I'm going to get bored and go eat my chicken if you don't do something right now."

That's totally a lie, and Trevor knows it. Skyler's not going anywhere, even if he's impatient.

"Hmm," Trevor says, tapping a finger on Skyler's lower back like he's contemplating. "I don't think so. I think you're going to do what I say and stop being a brat, aren't you?"

Oh, fuck.

There was no way for Skyler to miss the shift to dominance in Trevor's tone, and his cock jerks at the thought of what Trevor might do to him.

They don't play games like this too often—mostly because Trevor usually can't stop himself from being super soft with him and giving him everything he asks for immediately.

But sometimes Skyler asks for this. Usually he just wants it for fun. And then there are other times when letting Trevor take control of him helps him get out of his head if it's too full of self-doubts and other people's opinions for him to think properly.

Right now it seems like Trevor's the one who's in the mood for it. Maybe it's because he just came home from work, from a day of being in charge, and that boss energy has carried over. Whatever the reason, Skyler is definitely on board.

He jumps when there's another slap to his ass.

This is followed by the rhythmic sound of nails clacking against the floor as Stella wisely flees the room.

"I asked you a question, baby."

Holy hell. How does Trevor manage to call him baby and still give his words a dominating edge?

Skyler's brain scrambles to remember what the question was as Trevor slaps one ass cheek, then the other, following that one up with a squeeze and giving his ass a little jiggle.

"Oh, um, I—"

"Are you going to do what I say?" Trevor interrupts his floundering.

"Yes!" he agrees quickly. "Yes, I will. Yup. Anything you say."

Trevor chuckles at his enthusiastic answer. And Skyler realizes that making him answer was more than a simple display of dominance. It was Trevor's way of checking that Skyler was up for something like this. Having safely determined that, Trevor uses a firm hand between Skyler's shoulder blades to press his chest down harder on top of the counter. "Don't move," he says.

Skyler's pretty sure he's never had a thought of moving in his life.

He feels the loss of Trevor's body heat as Trevor steps away from him and over to the side where Skyler can't see. He listens intently to the sound of a drawer opening and Trevor rifling through it, unsure what he could be looking for.

When Trevor steps back into view, he's holding a medium-sized, mint-green silicone spatula.

Skyler gasps, jolting up to a standing position. "Oh my god, no! I cook with that!"

"That's what the dishwasher is for," Trevor says with a gentle laugh.

Wrinkling his nose, Skyler mutters, "It just seems wrong."

"Do you not want me to?" Trevor asks seriously, giving the spatula a light test slap into his palm.

All Skyler's concerns about whether this is sanitary are forgotten at the *thwack.*

He gulps in anticipation.

Yeah. He wants, he wants, he wants.

He gives a nod, and the only word he manages to say is, "Please."

"Please what?"

Taking a deep breath to get himself together and hopefully stop from coming on the spot, he adds, "Please do it. I want it."

Trevor grins wickedly. "Then you'd better get back over that counter."

Skyler hurries to comply, spinning around and bending down, bracing his forearms on the marble. His cockhead nudges the side again, and he suspects he's leaving a smear of precum, but he'll worry about cleaning later. He needs this now.

Trevor's hands come to Skyler's hips, gently urging them backward a bit so that his hip bones aren't pressed to the edge of the counter and his cock is no longer in danger of hitting into the side. "There, stay like that," Trevor says. "I promise I won't hit you too hard, okay, baby? I don't want you to hurt yourself on the counter."

Skyler smiles to himself. *Soft, soft, soft.* His husband is the softest.

When the first strike lands on his ass, he instantly reconsiders that sentiment. That was *not* soft. But he liked it.

There's a pause, in which Trevor is probably waiting to see if he'll object, but *nope.* No objections here.

Trevor hums like he's fascinated before hitting him again. Then he rubs over Skyler's ass cheek, spreading the warmth. "It's already making you red, baby. Are you okay?"

"*Mmm,* more," Skyler moans out his request.

Obligingly, Trevor removes his hand from Skyler's ass and gives him another few light thwacks with the spatula.

"So pretty," he hears Trevor murmur, almost to himself, as he rubs Skyler's hot skin again.

Skyler squirms, wiggling his ass in an attempt to ask for more.

It works.

Suddenly, Trevor's raining down blows, alternating cheeks and switching up spots without pausing to rub him anymore. The heat quickly builds until Skyler can no longer think. His mind goes foggy as his whole being narrows down to the fire on his ass cheeks and the smooth, cool marble against his chest and face.

"So good for me, baby," Trevor tells him. "You take this so well. Take whatever I give you so well."

Yes. He does. He will. Always.

Anything Trevor gives him is always what he needs.

The hits eventually slow, gentle, letting his racing heart start to calm. And then a sharp strike lands right at the bottom of his cheek where his ass meets his thigh. It lights him up again, makes him burn and want.

Trevor hits the same spot on the other cheek, and even though Skyler expects it this time, his hips jerk forward of their own accord, his body trying to escape even though he doesn't want to.

When Trevor goes back to hitting the meatier parts of his ass, he creates a steady rhythm. Not too slow, not too fast. Not too gentle, not too hard. It's just perfect for making Skyler's mind go blissfully empty again.

Like this, he has no room to worry about the responsibility of being the first gay Disney prince. He can just let his mind and body relax in the floaty, hazy place where all his edges feel fuzzy.

All he needs to do is be good for Trevor. For his husband. His everything.

He's not sure how long it takes him to notice after Trevor stops spanking him. But when he slowly lifts his cheek from the countertop and glances back at Trevor, Trevor is watching him with loving, adoring, ocean blue eyes.

"Hi, baby," Trevor whispers, as if Skyler's waking up from sleep.

He wasn't asleep though. He was here. Simply floating under Trevor's care.

"How's it feel?" Trevor asks.

As Skyler mentally assesses his body, the feeling of heat on his ass floods back in. He knows without checking that his dick is still hard as a rock, and now that he's aware of it again, he's also aware of how desperately he needs to come.

"Feels good," he says. "So good. But I need to come. Please. Please make me come."

"I will, baby," Trevor assures him. "But remember I said that I wanted to eat you? I still do. I just needed to heat up my dinner first."

Skyler isn't sure if he's going to laugh or cry. But he doesn't have time to do either before Trevor is back behind him and sinking to his knees on the kitchen floor.

"Oh god," Skyler says as Trevor's strong hands hold his ass cheeks apart.

And then he can't say anything else, because Trevor's tongue is licking at his rim, tasting him, teasing him.

Pulling his mouth away, Trevor says, "You cooked me such a good dinner, baby."

This time Skyler does laugh. He can't help it, despite how turned on he is.

Because this is ridiculous. His husband is ridiculous and wonderful and hot and *fuck*.

"Pretty sure you cooked it," he gasps out as Trevor's tongue spears inside his hole.

Trevor's noise of agreement is buried between Skyler's ass cheeks. As he eats Skyler's ass like a meal, Trevor brings his hands down to wrap around the backs of Skyler's thighs. He uses them as handles to pull Skyler farther backward against his face, and Skyler's not sure how Trevor can breathe like this.

Then Trevor slowly drags his nails down Skyler's thighs while he licks and sucks at his hole, and all the different sensations are the most delicious torture. Skyler's legs start to shake when Trevor lets go of them.

Using one hand to hold Skyler's ass open for him, Trevor brings the other around to the front of Skyler's hip. "If I touch your dick, are you going to come?"

"*Yesss*," Skyler breathes out.

Trevor hums. "Then I'll wait. Want you to come while I'm fucking you."

Skyler whimpers as Trevor's attention goes back to his ass. That's all he can do. He might cry if the fucking doesn't happen soon.

After another minute, Trevor stops what he's doing and releases Skyler, who sags against the counter, trying to keep himself up and not sink to the floor on his jelly legs.

"Stay," Trevor commands. Then he swiftly walks out of the room.

He's probably going for the stash of lube they keep hidden in the living room, since it's closer than going upstairs to their bedroom. Honestly, they should probably just keep some in the kitchen too, because it's not like this is the first time they've fucked in here. And Skyler's sure it won't be the last.

Especially not if Trevor keeps coming home from work with this kind of appetite.

A sense of relief washes over him when Trevor returns holding the bottle, because Skyler knows he's going to get fucked now. And he'll likely come as soon as Trevor is inside him. After that, he doesn't care what happens. His throbbing cock is all he can focus on at this moment.

And the heat on his ass. That's still there, hard to ignore now. And he loves it. It heightens the feelings of everything else.

After squirting some lube onto his fingers, Trevor drops the bottle on the counter beside Skyler's head, then he brings his hand down to Skyler's ass. He prods gently at Skyler's hole with one finger, and Skyler pushes his ass back in a desperate attempt to get that finger inside him pronto.

"Come on," he urges, sighing happily when Trevor's finger slips past his rim. "More. Hurry. I'm ready. You can fuck me now."

He's not even sure what he's saying, but it's true. He gets fucked often enough that he doesn't need much prep. When Trevor fingers him, it's more for the pure pleasure of it than anything else. But right now, his cock is painfully hard, and the pleasure is more like torture.

"I know I can fuck you now," Trevor says, in an infuriatingly casual tone. "I can also make you wait some more if I want to, because I'm in charge, aren't I?"

He punctuates his words with quick thrusts of his finger in and out of Skyler's hole, and it feels like every nerve ending in Skyler's body is on fire now. He's going to combust, but he's still trying to be good. Trying so hard to wait for Trevor's cock inside him, because that's what Trevor wanted. But he might not make it.

Draping himself over Skyler's back, Trevor gives him a kiss that's awkward from this angle but still so good. His finger keeps working inside Skyler's ass like magic and torture and too much and not enough.

As Trevor pulls away, Skyler looks into his eyes and whispers, "Please. I can't . . ."

He has trouble getting his words out, but Trevor understands him anyway. He always does.

"Hey, hey, hey, it's okay," Trevor says, his free hand petting soothingly down Skyler's side. "You've been so good for me, baby. So perfect. Love you so much."

"Love you too."

"I'll take care of you, okay?"

Skyler nods, trusting him. And Trevor doesn't waste any more time. He eases his finger out of Skyler's hole, then rearranges Skyler's body so that he's not bent over the island quite as much, letting Skyler brace himself on his hands rather than his forearms. As Trevor guides Skyler's hips farther away from the edge, Skyler knows to bend his knees just a tad to put his ass at the right height because he's slightly taller than Trevor.

The sound of Trevor's zipper is such a sweet relief. There's a tiny sting when the head of Trevor's cock pops past Skyler's rim, but it fades almost immediately as Trevor slowly but surely slides himself all the way home. The feeling of finally being full—of having his husband inside him, of being connected this way—is all Skyler needs to feel sated.

And one more pump of Trevor's cock out and back in is all it takes for Skyler's own cock to kick and start spilling ropes of cum onto the kitchen floor.

"Baby," Trevor says. Amused, impressed, maybe something else.

Skyler doesn't care. He's still riding the high of his explosive orgasm.

Trevor doesn't stop fucking him, and Skyler doesn't expect him to. He wants Trevor to use his body to get himself off. But when Trevor surprises him by wrapping a hand around Skyler's softening cock—

"Wha-*nngh.*" Skyler's question gets strangled around a whine.

"I think you can come for me again."

Skyler shakes his head, though he's already thrusting mindlessly into Trevor's hand. It hurts, but in a good way. Like his ass and the spanking.

Fuck. He might be able to come again if he replays *that* in his mind.

Trevor's free hand comes up to Skyler's sternum, and he uses it to force him more upright. Skyler's legs tremble from the effort of keeping his knees bent. Or maybe it's still from the orgasm and the way Trevor's steadily trying to work another one out of him. Who knows.

His cock is hard again, but he's not sure about his ability to come again so quickly. Ten years ago, definitely. But they're not so young anymore.

"Let go, baby," Trevor rasps in his ear. "Stop thinking about it. Just feel."

He feels like he's crawling out of his skin. And yet that's somehow not a bad thing.

"God, your ass feels so good squeezing around my cock," Trevor tells him. "Like your body was made for me."

It was. It definitely was. But Skyler's not capable of words right now, so he just does his best to tighten his muscles purposefully around Trevor's cock, and he's rewarded with his husband's loud groan.

"So fucking hot, baby," Trevor says, his pelvis slapping against Skyler's ass as he thrusts harder and faster, not letting the heat on Skyler's skin fade. "You're so hot. Everybody wants you. Everybody. But they can't have you, can they?"

Skyler frantically shakes his head.

"No, they can't," Trevor continues. "Because only I get to have you, right, baby? *Mine. Mine. Mine.*"

"Yours," Skyler manages to mumble.

Trevor's nailing Skyler's prostate now with each thrust, and meanwhile, his hand skillfully works over Skyler's cock. When he moves his hand down to give Skyler's balls a light tug, a spark shoots up Skyler's spine, and he knows he's about to come again.

"Fuuuuck!" he shouts as Trevor's palm rubs in a circle over his cockhead.

His cock only releases a small spurt this time, but the sensation of his second orgasm is so powerful he feels it from the tips of his ears all the way down to his toes.

Trevor's arms around his body are the only things holding him up. It's even possible that he loses consciousness for a few seconds, but the next thing he knows, Trevor's hips are pressed against him as Trevor stills and comes inside his ass.

After gently pulling out of his hole, Trevor helps ease Skyler down to the floor, avoiding the messy spot. Skyler rests his head against the side of the island while Trevor jumps up to pour a glass of water. When he settles back on the floor with Skyler, Trevor urges him to take a few slow sips by tilting the glass up to his mouth.

Skyler can't move. He's not even sure he's breathing. He's probably dead. That must be it.

But what a way to go.

A short while later, as they're eating side by side at the dining room table, with Skyler's script between them so they can read lines together, Trevor says, "This chicken is good, but it would've been better if we didn't have to microwave it."

Skyler shoots him a glare. "I hate you."

Trevor only smiles back at him. "No, you don't."

With a sigh, Skyler concedes and says, "I love you." Because it's the damn truth. And his pleasantly sore ass won't let him forget it.

"Love you too," Trevor tells him. "And I know everyone will fall in love with Prince Freddie, because you're going to do such an amazing job in this role. It was basically written for you, wasn't it? And the world already loves Skyler James."

"But not as much as you do?" Skyler asks. His anxiety over performing this role perfectly has already started melting away.

"Exactly," Trevor answers.

JULY

SKYLER JAMES AND TREVOR BLUE HOST 4TH OF JULY PARTY AT THE COUPLE'S MALIBU HOME

TREVOR

WHEN TREVOR STEPS OUT TO THE POOL DECK, carefully carrying a glass pitcher of lemonade that Skyler insisted on making from fresh squeezed lemons, the backyard is loud and full of people. He brings the pitcher over to the poolside bar they rarely use and sets it down, hoping it'll stay cool for a while under the structure's small roof. The ice bin behind the bar is stocked with ice and a variety of alcoholic beverages, but Trevor figured he should bring out a non-alcoholic option for the kids and anyone not trying to get drunk already.

His eyes scan the large expanse of yard to the right of the pool area for his husband, and he's mildly surprised to find Skyler standing with a bunch of the guys. Because he, Jermaine, Noah, Hal, and Hal's cousin Mickey have formed an awkward sort of circle, and they're tossing a football back and forth to one another. Trevor knows this wouldn't be Skyler's first choice of activity, but he's sure Skyler just wanted to hang with the guys and didn't really care what they were doing.

Stella also apparently wanted to hang out with everyone but not participate, because she's belly up about six feet outside of the circle, completely ignoring the ball that's flying through the air. Laziest German Shepard ever.

As Trevor watches, Mickey sends the football Skyler's way. And even from a distance, Trevor clocks how Skyler's eyes widen in surprise and almost terror, like he didn't expect anyone would actually throw to him.

Jermaine, who's standing closest to Skyler, laughs when the ball soars past Skyler's clumsily outstretched hands and hits him in the shoulder before bouncing to the grass. Trevor's lips twitch, but he lovingly holds back any laughter at his husband's expense.

Skyler doesn't look too upset about his miss, but when he picks up the ball, he only attempts the easiest toss to Jermaine.

Deciding Skyler doesn't need rescuing yet, Trevor walks over to the edge of the pool. He squats down near where Mike and his sister Annie are perched on the pool's underwater ledge. They look relaxed as they're watching Annie's two kids swim.

"Hey, there's lemonade on the bar if the kids get thirsty," Trevor tells them.

"Thanks," Annie says. "And thanks for inviting us."

"Of course. Sky was thrilled to host everyone. He was preparing food all day yesterday."

Mike snorts out a laugh. "Yeah, I'm still shocked he agreed to let me man the grill."

"Me too," Trevor admits.

Skyler is usually reluctant to relinquish cooking duties, but simple stuff like burgers and hot dogs aren't his forte. Who knows what he would've ended up making for everyone if he didn't agree to Mike's plan. Of course, he had to compensate by throwing together four different kinds of dip and about seven side dishes.

Trevor makes his way around to the other side of the pool where Layla is in her bikini, fully reclined on a lounger, sunglasses shielding her eyes. It was lucky she was able to take time off at the hospital to fly in from New York, since she isn't often able to do that on more major holidays. Skyler is thrilled that she's staying with them for a few days, and Trevor loves it too.

In the lounger next to Layla's, Megan has the exact same vibe going on, so Trevor decides not to disturb them. He turns toward Oli, who's sitting in one of the loungers that are under the shade of the house's awning, with Emma bouncing on his lap.

"Need anything?" Trevor asks as he walks over.

"Nah, I'm good," Oli says, taking one of Emma's little hands and having her wave at Trevor. "I wanna take Emma in the water, but Megan said I can't do it without her."

"Absolutely not!" Megan calls out.

Trevor laughs as Oli yells back at her, "I know how to put her in the big floaty thing!"

There's no response from Megan, but Oli sighs, obviously accepting that he's still not allowed to take his own daughter into the pool. "I swear I'm a responsible parent," he grumbles.

"We all know you are," Trevor tells him. But still, he thinks Megan's decision is probably wise.

Trevor sits sideways on the lounger next to Oli's, and as they chat, Jermaine's friend Chauncey, who's a DJ in New York, comes out of the house. He's shirtless and in a pair of turquoise swim trunks that are covered in pink flamingos. They look like something Skyler would wear if they were much shorter.

Chauncey and Jermaine flew in this morning and are staying in one of the guest wings. They were going to get a hotel, but Skyler convinced them to stay with him and Trevor. The house is more than big enough to accommodate the two of them and Layla.

Speaking of Layla, Trevor doesn't miss the way Chauncey's eyes linger on her as he walks around to the other side of the pool. He sits on the edge and puts his feet in, but his head casually swivels a couple more times in Layla's direction.

Layla was chatting his ear off earlier when they met, and Trevor could sense a potential vibe. Good thing Layla's staying in her own wing of the house. While Skyler understands that his sister is an adult who can make her own decisions, Trevor has a feeling he might be weirded out if she hooks up with one of his friend's friends.

He'd never ask her not to do it though. Skyler doesn't try to tell other people how to live their lives.

After catching up with Oli, Trevor heads across the yard to the football circle—either to join or to pull Skyler away if he's had enough of pretending to be sporty—and that's when he's hit with the realization of how happy he is right now. This party was Skyler's idea, and he was the one so excited to host it. Trevor was on board, but he didn't realize how much he'd truly love having all these people at his home.

Skyler coming back into his life brought along such a change from the way he'd been living before, when he spent all those depressing years pretty much alone. Sure, half of the people here are Trevor's friends as much as they are Skyler's, and he could've had them in his life back then whether he was with Skyler or not. But, in a way, he chose the loneliness before—maybe even needed it.

And now things are different. *He's* different.

Letting himself love Skyler again, not being afraid of it, unlearning all the bullshit the entertainment industry taught him . . . that lead him here. To living a full life, out in the sunshine, surrounded by people who care.

He's not alone. He has friends who are like family, and he has the one man who is everything to him.

The man who just successfully threw a football across the circle to Hal and is now doing an adorably ridiculous happy dance in his tiny red shorts.

Trevor laughs, stepping up behind Skyler and putting a hand on his shoulder. Skyler jumps a mile and whips around to face him. "Having fun?" Trevor asks.

The happiest smile spreads across Skyler's face as he leans in to give Trevor a quick kiss. Then he announces proudly, "I threw a ball, and it went where I meant it to!"

"I saw." Trevor gives his hip a squeeze.

"That was cool," Skyler says, leaning into Trevor's touch. In a stage-whisper, he adds, "But I think I'd like to be done now."

Jermaine obviously hears him, because he shakes his head and lets out a short laugh.

From across the circle, Noah yells to Trevor, "Are you playing?"

"Sorry, not right now," he calls back. "I'm gonna steal this one here"—he tugs on Skyler's hand—"to help me bring out some snacks."

Skyler giggles as he lets Trevor pull him away from the group and back toward the house. "My hero."

Since he might as well actually utilize Skyler's help, Trevor leads him inside. In the kitchen, he gathers some of the food while Skyler hops up onto the island and swings his long legs back and forth, not exactly being helpful.

"Gonna give me a hand with this, baby?" Trevor asks.

"Only if you give me a kiss first," Skyler says playfully.

Well, that's a very easy price to pay.

Trevor walks over to stand between Skyler's legs. Skyler's tiny shorts have ridden up, exposing the full lion head tattoo that sits indecently high on his left thigh, as well as the smattering of tattoos on his right one. Enjoying the view of all that skin, Trevor places his hands on both of Skyler's thighs and gives them a squeeze.

As Skyler leans down, Trevor tilts his head up to meet him for a kiss. He intends for it to be a quick one, but apparently his husband has other plans.

Skyler wraps a hand around the back of Trevor's neck when he tries to pull away, keeping him in place and their lips locked. When Skyler licks into Trevor's mouth, Trevor can't help the way his fingers dig a bit deeper into the muscles of Skyler's thighs. He sneaks his fingertips under Skyler's shorts and lets them explore a little higher.

Honestly, it can't be too comfortable for Skyler to keep his torso bent down like this, but he wraps his legs around Trevor's middle, indicating his desire to prolong this impromptu makeout session. So Trevor continues roaming his fingers along Skyler's skin, focusing on his sensitive inner thighs now. In response, a tiny, pleased sound slips past Skyler's lips as they kiss.

Trevor sucks Skyler's bottom lip into his mouth as Skyler's nails rake gently down his back over his T-shirt. Abandoning Skyler's thighs, Trevor slips his hands up underneath Skyler's tank top. He splays them out around Skyler's sides and travels up until his thumbs can graze across Skyler's nipples. Skyler shudders and nips at Trevor's lip.

Before they get too carried away, Trevor reluctantly forces himself to pull back. Skyler whines as they separate and attempts to reel Trevor back in, but Trevor moves too fast. "We have guests out there," he reminds him.

"Yeah, but they're *out there*." Skyler is still trying to reach for Trevor. "And we're in here."

Trevor shakes his head in amusement. "Anyone could walk inside. And besides, you don't want to be a rude host, do you?" Fully expecting Skyler's dirty look, he adds more seriously, "I know you want to spend time with everyone."

Huffing, Skyler hops off the counter. "Yeah, yeah. Of course, I do. What do you need me to carry?"

Trevor points at a platter of crackers, veggies, and dips, and when Skyler goes to grab it, Trevor takes a second to adjust his shorts. They're fitting tighter than they were when the two of them walked in here. Skyler smirks when he turns back and catches him, but Trevor cuts off whatever dirty proposition is sure to come next.

"Don't even try it, baby. Let's go."

As they're setting up the snacks outside, Skyler asks Trevor, "Jasper's still coming, right?"

"Oh yeah, he said he was." Frowning, Trevor pulls his phone out of his pocket to check the time. And then he feels like an ass when he sees the text from Jasper.

So . . . how do I actually get IN your place?

It's from five minutes ago.

"Shit." Why didn't Jasper call him? "I think he might be at the gate."

Ignoring Skyler's unimpressed look, Trevor says he'll be right back, then dashes into the house, calling Jasper as he goes.

"Uh, hey," Jasper answers uncertainly.

"Hi, I'm so sorry. Are you here?"

"Yeah. At least, I think I'm at the right place. But there's a gate?" Jasper says that last part like a question.

"Totally my fault," Trevor admits. "I should've given you the code ahead of time."

Jasper chuckles, but it sounds more awkward than amused. "No big deal. I mean, I'm a little worried that some cops are gonna pull up and arrest me for loitering outside a celebrity home, but . . ." He gives another awkward chuckle as he lets the sentence hang.

Mentally smacking himself, Trevor gives Jasper the code and directions for opening the gate. "Just follow the driveway all the way up until you see the main house and all the cars. Everyone's out back, but it's easier if you come through the house. I'll meet you at the front door."

"Cool, thanks," Jasper says before hanging up.

Trevor heads to the front of the house, feeling like a jerk. He invited Jasper because the guy mentioned he had no plans over the holiday weekend, and because Trevor wants to get to know him better. He wants Jasper to know he can trust him. To understand that Trevor's here to help him build his career, not to take advantage of him.

The album they recorded came out great. His sound guys are just working on a few things in post-production, and then it'll be ready for release. But Trevor understands that dropping a newbie's album onto the scene isn't enough to get them noticed, no matter how good it is. Jasper's success as an artist is going to come down to his own personality and stage presence, so his first few live performances will be crucial.

Trevor's sure that if Jasper can learn to fully let himself go when all eyes are on him, to not let the pressure or the fear of making mistakes get to him—and to not worry about the inevitable abuse he'll get from some haters—he's going to grab people's attention. He'll captivate them the way he did with Trevor, with his voice and his earnest lyrics.

As he opens the front door to step outside, Trevor hears someone hustling up behind him. He turns his head and smiles at Skyler. "He'll be here in a sec. You didn't have to come with me."

"But I wanted to be the first to meet him!"

"I don't want him to feel overwhelmed or out of place or anything."

Skyler's grin is huge and only a tiny bit worrisome. "Don't worry. I'm sure we'll become friends right away."

Trevor laughs at that, because yeah, Skyler's so nice he could probably make friends with a brick wall. But he has a feeling Jasper's more nervous about meeting Skyler than he's let on. Jasper has spoken more than once about how much he respects Skyler as an artist, and how much of an inspiration Skyler's been for him with his own music.

They watch as a dark green beat-up car pulls into their large circular drive, and then it takes Jasper a minute to get out. He's wearing black basketball shorts, which is quite the deviation from his usual edgy style. But the shorts reveal that his left leg is entirely covered with tattoos. It's the opposite of his arms, where the ink is on his right and the left one is bare. And Trevor's allowed to admit that's pretty hot, right?

What makes the sight of Jasper in sportswear even more jarring, though, is the way he's paired the basketball shorts with his signature leather jacket. Like he attempted a casual style but got caught up halfway. It's not a look someone would likely go for on purpose.

Skyler lets out a tiny sigh. "Oh boy. We'll need to fix this man's fashion sense, stat."

"Leave him alone," Trevor defends quickly as Jasper approaches them. "I don't think all this is his scene."

"Clearly," Skyler says. But there's absolutely no hint of anything mean behind it. He's probably already coming up with a plan for how he'll make Jasper feel more comfortable.

Jasper's eyes widen as Skyler swiftly slides past Trevor to greet him. Skyler introduces himself in that endearing way of his, where he pretends like he's not famous and the person he's introducing himself to doesn't already know who he is. Jasper looks a little caught off guard by this, but he shakes Skyler's hand and then thanks him and Trevor for inviting him.

Trevor lets Skyler take the lead in ushering Jasper through the house, and thankfully Skyler only makes a bit of small talk while they walk, rather than immediately asking for Jasper's whole life story. Which Trevor is sure he's dying to do.

At the back of the house, Skyler stops in front of the doors to the outside and faces Jasper. "You know, you'll probably be hot with that jacket on," he says, keeping his tone casual. "We could hang it up in here if you want." He points to a set of hooks on the wall.

Rubbing one of the jacket sleeves between his fingers, Jasper says, "Right. Yeah. I guess I just felt weird without it." He shrugs awkwardly but holds Skyler's gaze. "I know I don't exactly fit in here with all you famous people. I almost brought my guitar to blend in, but then I thought it might make me look like a douche instead."

Trevor feels a pang of sympathy for him. With the band, he and the rest of the guys gained fame absurdly fast, so they didn't really experience imposter syndrome or anything like that. When they attended events and met other celebrities, everyone was interested in talking to them and treated them like they belonged.

"Oh!" Skyler exclaims, his face lighting up. "You totally could've brought your guitar. But it's okay, I've got plenty for you to use. I'd love to play with you!"

Jasper looks even more confused now than when Skyler introduced himself to him. "You would? Why?"

Skyler laughs. "Trevor keeps talking about how talented you are! I've heard some of your stuff, and I think it would be fun." Shaking his head, he adds, "And there's not a bunch of famous people here. It's just us and the rest of the guys and some other family."

Trevor rolls his eyes, because "the rest of the guys" are most definitely famous people, along with Trevor and Skyler. But obviously, to Trevor and Skyler, they're just their friends. Their family.

"Uh, okay," Jasper says as he shrugs out of his jacket. Trevor's not sure if the okay is him agreeing to play some music with Skyler, or him pretending to agree with Skyler's assessment that he's not about to meet a bunch of other famous people.

Skyler holds out his hand to take the jacket, then hangs it up for him. "You brought something to swim in, right?" he asks. "If not, you can borrow something from me."

"Or me," Trevor jumps in. Because there's no way Jasper will want to wear one of Skyler's skimpy pairs of swimwear.

Jasper shakes his head. "No, it's okay. I've got shorts on under my . . . shorts. Thanks, though."

"Okay, perfect." Skyler slides an arm around his shoulders. "Let's go introduce you to everyone, and then if you want, we can come back inside and I'll show you my music room,"

"Oh. Yeah. That'd be cool." There's genuine interest evident in Jasper's voice now.

With that settled, Skyler all but drags him outside. And even though Jasper still looks slightly apprehensive, Trevor knows he's in good hands, so he leaves them to it.

He heads over to the bar area, where Noah's munching on some food. "Hey. Having fun?"

Noah doesn't answer that. His disgruntled gaze is focused over Trevor's shoulder. "I didn't know *he* was coming."

"Yeah, you did. I told you I invited him."

With a huff, Noah looks away from wherever Jasper is and grabs a strip of red pepper off his plate, dragging it through a glob of Skyler's homemade hummus. "I didn't think he'd actually come. I mean, he doesn't know anyone."

Trevor gives him a warning look. "He knows us."

Why does Noah have such a hard time being nice to Jasper?

Noah shoves the veggie in his mouth and starts chomping loudly, which Trevor takes as a suggestion to change the topic of conversation.

"Have you heard from your parents lately?" he asks.

But this might not be the best topic either, because Noah scowls for a second before he schools his face into a more neutral expression. "Nah. It's been a couple months. They're still blogging, though. I read they were in Switzerland last week."

Trevor wants to say something about how much it sucks that his parents have practically forgotten about him since they took off to explore the world almost a year ago with no end date in sight. Especially considering it was Noah paying off their mortgage years ago that allowed them to save up for the indefinite leaves of absence from their jobs. And he knows Noah added what must have been a sizable chunk to their savings account when they told him about their travel idea, which helped them out some more.

But since he's sure Noah doesn't want to get into a conversation like that today, all he says is, "Hope they liked the Alps."

Noah's expression basically tells Trevor to fuck off, so he reaches out to give Noah's shoulder a squeeze, keeping his hand there for a few extra seconds before letting go.

"I'm here if you ever wanna talk, man."

Noah simply nods, then resumes eating. But it seems like at least some of the tension has left his body. Trevor leaves him alone after that, wandering around to check on everyone else. Chauncey is throwing a tennis ball for Stella, who has finally overcome her laziness and is now eagerly sprinting back and forth across the yard. The girls are still sunbathing. And Hal and Mickey have congregated around Mike at the grill. Trevor asks if Mike needs anything, but Mike salutes him with his beer and says he's got it handled.

That leaves Trevor free to join the conversation Skyler and Jasper are having with Oli and Jermaine. Skyler's still glued to Jasper's side like a cross between an excitable puppy and an overprotective parent. But Jasper is smiling as he talks about his album with the guys, which Trevor loves to see.

Noah joins the group a minute later. Thankfully, he refrains from making any snarky comments at Jasper's expense. He doesn't actually say much at all, though. And Trevor doesn't like seeing his friend in this moody funk, but he can't really do anything about it right now.

After everyone eats what Mike grilled up, Skyler convinces Jasper to play guitar and sing with him. They perch themselves on the edge of a couple Adirondack chairs in the lawn, and Trevor takes a seat to watch. So do Oli, Megan, and Annie. Annie's kids are busy playing with Stella a few feet away, but they do start singing when they recognize one of Skyler's most popular songs.

Jasper seems starstruck again as he sings with Skyler. But aside from that, he looks just as much in his element as Skyler does.

Watching the two of them play together, Trevor grows even more sure in his gut instinct about Jasper's stardom potential. Someday the world will know Jasper Bell's name. Trevor's going to do everything he can to make sure that happens.

A little later, when Trevor makes a trip inside to grab more alcohol and change into his swim trunks, Skyler follows him. And apparently, Skyler agrees about Jasper's talent, because he's chattering excitedly about how cool it would be if Jasper opened for him on his next tour.

"Let's worry about getting his album out there first," Trevor tells him, heading for the fridge. He's not going to mention how Skyler hasn't seriously started working on *his* next album yet, so planning for his next tour is a bit far off. At least this time, Skyler's label is handling his break better. They're not totally up his ass about it yet.

Key word being *yet*. But it feels like Skyler's gotten so big that everyone's confident his fanbase will wait, and probably grow, even if he takes longer between album releases.

"Maybe I'll find another up and coming band to open too. Like an all-girl band with a lesbian lead singer," Skyler goes on, ignoring Trevor in his enthusiasm. "Wouldn't that be awesome? I'll name the tour Queers on Tour, or something like that."

At this, Trevor sets a case of beer on the counter and turns back to look at his husband. Whether this idea is a legitimate one or just something Skyler's amusing himself with, Trevor can't help but smile at him. This man is too damn sweet.

Skyler cocks his head questioningly. "What?"

"Nothing," Trevor says, unable to tame his smile.

"I know how incredibly lucky I am to have reached the position I'm in now," Skyler tells him. "And in being able to come out without hurting my career at all. So if I have the ability to help other queer artists, I want to use it. Boost them up so that maybe they don't have to go through all the hoops I went through to get here."

Trevor continues gazing fondly at his husband as he tries to come up with the words to say how amazing it is that Skyler cares so deeply about stuff like this.

"What?" Skyler asks again, tugging self-consciously at a strand of wavy hair that's slipped out of his messy bun.

"Have I ever told you that your heart is the sexiest thing about you?"

A grin spreads slowly across Skyler's face. "Oh yeah? Are you sure it's the *sexiest* thing? I mean, I have so many other parts to choose from, and I know you appreciate them all."

With a laugh, Trevor tells him. "I definitely do, baby."

"So where do all the rest of my parts rank after my heart?" Skyler asks playfully, stepping closer until he's got Trevor caged in against the counter. "I'm guessing my ass is next, but I know how much you like my dick too."

As if Trevor might need a reminder of that particular body part, Skyler rocks his hips forward, pressing his groin into Trevor's. His growing erection is already blatantly obvious, thanks to the thin material of his shorts.

Trevor grinds against him in return, winding a hand around the back of Skyler's neck to pull him in close enough to kiss him. When he licks at the seam of Skyler's lips, Skyler opens his mouth for him, inviting Trevor's tongue inside. They kiss and rub and grab at each other for a few glorious moments before Skyler pulls away.

"I almost forgot about my mouth," he says. "Know you like that too."

"Love your mouth," Trevor agrees. "Your lips always taste like coconut."

Skyler chuckles. "That's chapstick."

"I know." Trevor yanks him back in for another kiss. "Love kissing you," he utters against Skyler's lips. "Gonna kiss you for the rest of my life."

"You'd fucking better, or I'll be upset," Skyler says before going in for more.

Trevor's impossibly hard now. And he's almost regretting starting this, because they can't finish it. They need to get back to their party.

When Skyler breaks off the kissing this time, he's got a wicked gleam in his eyes. "But you like my mouth for other things too, right?" he asks. And he might have managed to pull off sounding perfectly innocent—if only Trevor didn't know this man so fucking well.

Before Trevor can answer, Skyler is dropping to his knees on the hard kitchen floor and tugging down the waistband of Trevor's shorts.

"Woah, hold on, baby." Trevor reaches down to grip Skyler's shoulders. "We can't do this now."

"Why not?" Skyler asks, smirking up at him as he continues slowly lowering Trevor's shorts all the way to his ankles.

Having still not changed into his swim trunks, Trevor's wearing a pair of black boxer briefs underneath, and his hard cock strains helplessly at the fabric. Skyler mouths at it, making Trevor groan softly. Just feeling the warm breath there is enough to have Trevor forgetting to give him an answer.

He should tell Skyler to stop. He should remind him about all their guests outside. But all he manages is one more half-hearted, murmured protest as Skyler peels the briefs away and immediately darts out his tongue to lick at the head of Trevor's cock.

Trevor's hips jerk forward without his permission, and at the same time, Skyler opens his mouth, which sends Trevor's cock sliding a few inches past Skyler's lips. Skyler moans sweetly, like Trevor just fed him a delicious treat.

Trying to get control of himself, Trevor slides his fingers through Skyler's hair until they get caught up on the bun. Then he takes a deep breath. He's torn between holding Skyler's head there, mouth on his cock, or tugging him off.

"Baby," he says when he finds his words. "We should save this for later. We can't—"

He's cut off in surprise as Skyler lets Trevor's cock slip from his mouth. When he glances down, he finds Skyler gazing up at him with lust in his green eyes.

Skyler licks his bottom lip and says, "I'll make it quick, I promise. Please. I need to have you now. Wanna make you feel good."

With that, he slides his mouth back over Trevor's cock, not stopping until he's taken it all down his throat and his nose is pressed to Trevor's neatly trimmed pubic hair.

"*Fuuuck*," Trevor groans, though he tries to keep it quiet. It's not like anyone can hear from outside, but still. They shouldn't be doing this right now, right here.

They're not the same horny twenty-year-olds who couldn't control themselves while the band was on tour. Back then, they'd gotten caught so many times hooking up on tour buses and in dressing rooms, and it didn't really phase them. But now they're adults hosting a party. They should be outside with their guests—not inside with their dicks out.

Though, Trevor supposes, his dick is technically covered right now. That's something, isn't it?

No.

He can't think straight while Skyler is swallowing around him and doing things with his tongue that Trevor can't even comprehend at the moment. Skyler lightly rolls Trevor's balls in his palm, and Trevor has to hold on to the edge of the countertop behind him to keep his knees from buckling.

"Fuck, yes, so good. So good, baby," he praises as Skyler expertly works him over. "Love you on your knees for me."

When Skyler moans in response, the vibrations travel up Trevor's cock and seem to go all the way up his spine. Trevor really can't remember why they weren't supposed to be doing this. But then, right as he feels the tingle in his balls that lets him know he's about to come, the universe decides to give him a giant reminder.

Loud footsteps clomp into the kitchen, and a voice yells, "Ah, *shit*, fucking hell!"

Trevor's eyes shoot upward and widen at Hal, who is standing there frozen, partially covering his eyes, but also staring in horror through his spread fingers.

And to Trevor's own horror, it's too late to stop the inevitable.

Skyler starts to pull off Trevor's cock at the interruption, but Trevor's balls draw up tight, and he quickly shoves Skyler's head back down. Because coming down Skyler's throat in front of his bodyguard has got to be a better option than coming all over his face.

Skyler sputters a bit in surprise, but he takes it, swallowing everything down. Then he just stays there—on his knees with Trevor's softening cock still in his mouth—while Trevor tries to recover his senses.

"Uh," Trevor says, eyes still locked awkwardly with Hal. "Can you, um, please leave?"

Hal rapidly nods his head. "Yup. Yeah. Right. I'll, uh, do that now. I was just gonna grab . . . I forgot. Doesn't matter. Yeah, I'll go." He starts backing out of the room and knocks into the door frame before he remembers to turn around.

Once he's out of sight, Trevor taps Skyler's shoulder and tells him, "All clear."

Skyler pulls off Trevor's cock, giving him a couple licks to clean him up. Then he wipes his mouth as he stands. "Well, that was . . . exciting."

Trevor attempts to give him a dark look, but it's hard to be upset with his husband right after he made him come. Even if it was with an audience. "I think we got enough of that kind of excitement in the old days, didn't we?" he asks as he pulls up his briefs and shorts. "We don't really need any more of it."

Smiling sheepishly, Skyler says, "Yeah, I didn't actually expect to get caught. I'm sorry."

"I guess I can forgive you, baby." Trevor winds an arm around Skyler's waist to pull him in closer. Feeling Skyler's erection nudging his hip, he laughs. "Seriously? That interruption wasn't enough to kill the mood for you?"

Skyler shrugs. "It did a little. But I can't help how horny you make me."

"Well, hate to break it to you, but you'll need to find a way to make that go down on your own. Because I am *not* risking getting caught again."

"That's fine," Skyler tells him. "I'll just save it for fucking you later."

Trevor rolls his eyes, but he doesn't think that's meant to be a joke. "Come on. I'm gonna change into my trunks, and you can bring this out there." He taps the case of beer on the counter.

"Oh, no way," Skyler says, shaking his head. "You know they're all gonna give us shit. I'm not going out there alone. I'll wait for you."

That's fair, Trevor supposes. Although he still maintains that this indiscretion was mostly Skyler's fault. Not that Trevor tried too hard to stop him.

He runs upstairs and changes as quickly as he can before rejoining Skyler in the kitchen. As Skyler picks up the beer, he giggles loudly.

"What?" Trevor asks him.

"*Can you, um, please leave?*" Skyler mocks, clearly fighting to keep a straight face.

Trevor gives him a light shove. "Shut up. What was I supposed to say? I can't believe I let you do that with all these people here. You're a menace."

"But I'm your menace," Skyler says proudly.

"Yeah, you are," Trevor tells him. And he wouldn't have it any other way.

They do get a round of catcalls when they walk out back. Even the kids get in on it—though presumably, they have no real idea what's going on. But after embarrassing them, everyone quickly moves on.

Trevor wasn't sure if they'd see any fireworks tonight, but they end up with a decent view of some being set off farther down the coast. They're probably coming from the backyard of some other rich celebrity with too much money to blow.

Actually, Trevor's surprised that Skyler didn't want to set off their own display. Maybe he didn't think of it. But there's a good chance he's already mentally planning it for next year as he stares up at the bright colors, his hand clutched in Trevor's. Trevor pays more attention to the light dancing off his husband's gorgeous face than he does to the show in the sky.

By the time the fireworks stop, most of the adults are looking drunk, tired, or both. The kids, on the other hand, seem like they could party all night.

Seated on the end of a lounger, Trevor sips his beer and watches Skyler playing with them in the lit-up pool. Annie's kids are bobbing through the water, circling him like sharks, while Skyler holds Emma under her armpits and dips her tiny legs in and out of the water, to the baby's obvious delight.

Megan is nearby, but she's only paying a minimal amount of attention to the pool. It's funny how she didn't trust her own husband to take Emma in, but she trusts Skyler. Though it's easy to see why. Skyler is a natural with kids.

The baby's wearing inflatable arm bands, but Skyler's not using the giant floating contraption that Megan had her in earlier. He makes it look effortless as he takes care of Emma and keeps the other kids entertained. He gently warns the kids when they're splashing too close to the baby, and they listen to everything he says right away.

Seeing how happy Skyler is with all of them makes Trevor smile.

Layla must catch him as she plops down in a lounger beside him with a drink in her hand, because she says, "It's sickeningly adorable, right?"

Trevor chuckles. "I've always known he's good with kids, but he doesn't really get the chance to be around them like this too often. He must be loving it."

Layla hums thoughtfully. "You know, sometimes I think I must be adopted."

"What the hell?"

"Because *that*"—she tips her drink in the direction of the pool—"would be my worst nightmare. But Sky looks like he's having the time of his life."

Mostly to himself, Trevor says, "I wish I could give him that."

"Kids?" Layla asks, raising her eyebrows at him.

"Yeah . . ."

He and Skyler always used to talk about having a big family one day. But then everything fell apart. With them, with the band. And then there was Trevor's ex-wife and that whole disaster.

Since he and Skyler got back together, they haven't seriously discussed the topic. It sort of seems impossible at this stage of their lives and careers. But Trevor would bet anything that Skyler still wants kids.

"He'd be an amazing dad," he says wistfully.

Layla nods. "He definitely would. And so would you, because you're a total caretaker. Is that something you still want, though?"

She doesn't mention it, but Trevor suspects she's also remembering how Trevor's ex tricked him into thinking she was pregnant and lost the baby. But he's managed to let go of that pain.

Now all he wants is whatever Skyler wants. He'd give Skyler anything he asks for. But if Trevor takes a moment to consider it . . . Yeah, a big family with Skyler still sounds perfect.

"I'm going to interpret the dreamy expression on your face and the way you can barely take your eyes off Sky as a yes," Layla tells him.

"I don't know how we'd make it happen. But yeah, if he wants it, then I do too," Trevor admits.

Layla glances to the pool before looking back at Trevor. "I'm gonna be the coolest aunt ever." Wrinkling her nose, she adds, "Just don't ask me to babysit."

"Deal," Trevor says, clinking his beer bottle against her drink can.

As he continues watching Skyler having a blast in the pool, his mind begins dreaming up their potential future together, and what that might look like with a few kids running around here.

It's a really great image. And Trevor will do whatever it takes to make it happen for them.

For Skyler.

Because Skyler James deserves to have everything he's ever wanted.

AUGUST

SKYLER JAMES SPOTTED ARRIVING IN NEW YORK AHEAD OF BENEFIT SHOW

TREVOR

STUMBLING HIS WAY DOWNSTAIRS bleary-eyed at three a.m., Trevor debates whether he should brew an extremely strong pot of coffee and try to start his day stupidly early, or if he should just go back to bed after Skyler leaves. Skyler insisted Trevor could have stayed in bed entirely, of course, but Trevor ignored him. He wants to send his husband off with a kiss before his flight to New York. Even if that means rising hours before the sun.

Last night, while Skyler was packing, he started to get upset at the idea of spending the next few days in New York without Trevor. Originally, he had assured Trevor that it wasn't a big deal if Trevor stayed home to work, because Skyler was only supposed to be there for one night. But at the last minute, his agent talked him into also doing an interview while he's in the city, so now he's staying longer.

And unfortunately, Trevor has too many meetings lined up at work now. So even though he hates seeing Skyler upset, it was too late for Trevor to decide to go with him. Skyler understands that, but he was still pouting a little when they went to bed.

After spending all that time together on Skyler's tour last year—after being confined with each other night after night on planes and buses and in hotel rooms—you'd think Skyler would be cool with having some space and a few days apart. But the truth is, they both loved every minute of the time they got to spend together on the tour. They reveled in the freedom that came from coming out publicly as a couple, from no longer having to hide. And while the reporters following them like vultures got tiring, they never got sick of each other.

Trevor would have done a second year like that if Skyler had asked him to.

This year, though, with their separate schedules, Skyler has occasionally become clingy in the way he often was when they were younger. Not that Trevor ever minded it back then, and he doesn't now. It's just not who Skyler is anymore.

Skyler has so much to fill his time with outside of Trevor, between his career and his hobbies and his friends. So Trevor's started to wonder if there's something else going on now when he gets like this.

When Trevor joined Skyler on his tour, it felt like the best parts of the old days of being in the band together. Because while that era of their lives came with many challenges, they at least got to spend almost all of their time together. And now that they're no longer on the tour and they occasionally have to spend nights apart, the separation might remind Skyler of all those painful years they spent apart in between the breakup and getting back together.

Or maybe Trevor's projecting.

He certainly doesn't like being reminded of that miserable time in his life without Skyler. But he firmly believes they wouldn't have the relationship they have now if they hadn't been through that hard part in the past. And he knows their love will survive anything now, including sleeping in different beds for a few nights.

He wishes he could join Skyler in New York, but since he can't, the least he can do is crawl his ass out of bed at this ungodly hour to say goodbye.

He finds his husband in the kitchen, pouring coffee into a thermos that's mint green with white daisies on it. Skyler smiles when he sees Trevor, but he still seems upset. The dimples don't come out to play.

Wrapping his arms around Skyler's waist, Trevor kisses his cheek. "Good morning, baby."

"Not a very good one," Skyler mutters. "I don't wanna go."

"Come on." Trevor squeezes him tighter. "You know you want to be a part of the benefit show. It's for a good cause."

Skyler huffs. "Fine. I want to go. I just don't want to go alone."

"You'll have Mike with you," Trevor counters, which earns him a dark look.

"Not what I mean."

"I know. But you'll get to see Layla too, won't you? And hang out with Jermaine?"

Jermaine is also performing tonight, and he and Skyler already made plans to go out together after the show. Skyler got Layla on the guest list, so she'll be there to watch him, but she probably won't be able to hang out with them afterward, since she has to work early in the morning.

Skyler winds his arms around Trevor's neck and says, "Yeah, okay. That'll be fun. I'm just being dramatic."

Trevor pretends to gasp. "I'm shocked."

"Shut up," Skyler says, reaching down to smack his ass and then leaving his hand there, just cupping Trevor's ass cheek over his joggers.

Trevor carefully runs his fingers through Skyler's long hair, which is all the way down today, while Skyler lets him know he made a full pot of coffee in case Trevor wanted some. After thanking him with a kiss, Trevor tells him he's going to miss him.

This prompts a petulant, "Oh sure, you're gonna miss me, but you won't come with me."

It's Trevor's turn to fix Skyler with a look until Skyler relents.

"I'm sorry. You can ignore me. I know I'm being selfish. I'm happy that stuff with your label is going so well, even if it keeps you really busy lately."

"Well, pretty soon you'll be busy again with putting out another album, and you won't even notice if I'm not around," Trevor reminds him.

"Not true," Skyler says. Then his phone beeps, and he takes it out of the pocket of his sweatpants to check it. "Mike pulled the car up. I've gotta go."

Trevor cradles his face in one hand, rubbing his thumb along Skyler's cheekbone before kissing him one more time. "You're going to have so much fun at the show tonight. And I'll be watching from here."

The station is airing it live, so when it starts at nine p.m. in New York, it'll be six here. And Trevor is absolutely going to make sure he gets home from work in time to not miss anything.

"I'm gonna call you when it's done," Skyler tells him.

"You'll be too busy."

Skyler shakes his head. "Nonsense."

"Okay, baby." Trevor smiles fondly as he follows Skyler out of the kitchen.

At the front door, Trevor starts grabbing the bags Skyler left there, even though he knows Mike will be coming up to the door to take them. After stepping outside and handing them off, Trevor pulls Skyler in for just one more kiss. For real this time. Last one.

"I'll be waiting for your call. I love you."

Skyler tells him he loves him too, and he looks slightly more upbeat as he jogs to the car. Trevor watches Mike loop it around and head off in the dark down the winding driveway. Then Trevor tries not to groan as he turns back inside, still unsure if he should bother trying to get a few more hours of sleep.

THE SHOW WAS GREAT. It's not the first year the channel has hosted it, and not Skyler's first year participating. But it was Trevor's first year getting to watch Skyler in it without his heart breaking and being weighed down with regret. So that was nice.

He figures it'll take Skyler quite a bit of time to call him once the show goes off the air, but fifteen minutes after he turned off his TV, Trevor's phone rings.

"Hey," he answers.

There's a lot of noise in the background, but he can still hear the smile in Skyler's voice when he replies, "Hey, husband."

"You were great tonight," Trevor tells him.

"Thanks! Everyone was so good. I had so much fun!"

Trevor smiles, glad to hear Skyler sounding a lot happier than he was when he left this morning. "I'm glad, baby. Are you with Jermaine?"

"Yeah, we're leaving now to go to the afterparty," Skyler says, as Jermaine yells a greeting into the phone.

"Okay, I'll let you go."

"But I want to talk to you more," Skyler insists.

So Trevor tells him he can call again when he gets back to the apartment tonight if he's not too tired. Which Trevor fully expects him to be after a six-hour flight, a televised event, and some partying. But if it'll make Skyler feel better to know that he can call if he wants to, then Trevor will make sure he knows he can.

Of course, Skyler argues that Trevor will probably already be asleep, since he got up so early this morning. "And I know you'll need to wake up for work tomorrow too," he says. "I don't want to disturb you."

"Baby, don't even worry about that, okay? If I'm already asleep, I'll wake up for you. I *want* to." Truthfully, Trevor almost certainly *will* be asleep by the time Skyler's done hanging out with Jermaine. It's only nine now, and he's already fading fast. But he couldn't care less about how all this affects his sleep schedule. He'll always be there for his husband if he needs him.

And his words seem to make Skyler happy, so Trevor gets off the phone feeling good. What's one more night of too little sleep? He'll be fine.

Before he gets in bed, he makes sure to turn his phone's volume up as loud as it goes, and he just hopes his body's not so exhausted that he sleeps through the ringing. He doesn't want to break his promise.

It feels like he falls asleep as soon as his head hits the pillow, and the next thing he knows, he's being woken up by an obnoxious sound. He's groggy as he opens his eyes. It takes him a few more seconds to realize what's going on, but then he lunges for his phone and sits up in bed.

"Hey," he mumbles, his voice still coming alive.

"I'm sorry," is the first thing Skyler says. It's much quieter on his end of the line than it was earlier. "I knew I should've let you sleep instead of waking you."

"No, it's okay, baby," Trevor assures him. "I told you to. How was the rest of your night?"

Skyler proceeds to tell him all about what he and Jermaine got up to and fills him in on news from the other celebrities they hung out with. Trevor's happy to listen, though he briefly takes the phone from his ear to check the time. It's only a little after eleven. On any other night, he likely wouldn't have even been asleep yet, but getting up at three this morning did a number on him.

He leans over to pet Stella, who has taken full advantage of Skyler's absence by lying all sprawled out on the bed with him. Her back leg starts kicking in the air when he scratches the right spot on her belly.

While Skyler continues to talk, Trevor fights off a yawn, not wanting Skyler to hear it. He doesn't care that his body is pleading with him to go back to sleep. All he cares about is that Skyler had a good time and isn't going to be too lonely staying in the New York apartment without him.

Of course, as Skyler finishes recounting his night, Trevor catches how his excited tone starts to shift to a more subdued one.

"I'm glad you had fun, baby," Trevor tells him.

"It was fun while I was out with everyone, but now that I'm here in the apartment alone . . ." Skyler lets out a sad little sigh as he trails off.

Trevor immediately feels guilty, even though he knows that's not his husband's intention. "I know. But it's only a few nights, and then you'll be back here with me."

"Wish you were *here* with me."

Trevor sighs this time, but then he gets an idea. "Okay. What if you pretend I'm there with you?"

"*Pfft.* I know I'm whining, but I'm not a child," Skyler says. "I don't think that's going to work."

What Trevor has in mind is certainly *not* fit for a child. "I meant I'll help you get relaxed and feeling good, and I'll talk you through it as if I was there touching you," he explains.

"Talk me through . . . *Ohhh.* Yeah. *Yes.* Let's do that please."

Trevor chuckles softly. "So polite, baby. Are you in bed?"

An eager, "Mmhmm," is the only response he gets.

"Good. Can you sit up a bit? It doesn't have to be all the way. Just prop yourself up a little with some pillows and get comfortable. Give yourself room to spread your legs."

That last instruction may seem unnecessary, considering how big the bed is in that apartment. But Trevor has a feeling Skyler's lying on one side of it, being so used to sharing his beds with Trevor.

"Okay, I'm ready." Skyler's voice has gone soft already.

"Perfect," Trevor tells him. Then he gets himself situated and imagines what he would do if he really were there, with Skyler lounging on the bed looking all gorgeous for him. "Now I want you to put your thumb over your mouth. Use it to gently push down your bottom lip, then peek your tongue out to get your thumb a little wet for me."

He waits a few seconds, setting his own hand on his lower abdomen and letting his fingertips dip down under the waistband of his boxers. "Okay, baby. Imagine I'm there, I'm lying beside you. And imagine I'm the one touching you. I want you to take your thumb from your lips and move it across your jawline, then slowly slide it down your neck. Use just a little bit of pressure. Imagine it's me pressing kisses there."

There's a soft gasp on the other end of the line, and Trevor doesn't need to ask, but he does anyway. "Did you do it?"

"Yeah," Skyler replies breathlessly. Trevor can tell he's already turned on, even though they haven't done much of anything yet. But Skyler does have a great imagination. Just picturing Trevor in his mind doing this to him is probably turning him on way more than the actual physical sensations.

"Good job, baby. You're so good for me." These words elicit another gasp from Skyler. Loving that, Trevor slides his hand farther into his boxers to cup his soft dick before he continues. "Can you wet your thumb again for me?"

"Yes," Skyler is quick to say.

"Good. Now this time bring it down to your nipple. Circle it until it hardens into a little peak for me."

The quiet moan tells him Skyler is following his instructions.

"Now flick your thumb over it a few times," he says.

The moan that follows is louder this time.

"Do you wanna do the same thing with the other one for me?" Trevor asks. "Lick your thumb again first." He waits until he hears another moan before he asks, "Do you like how that feels, baby? Do you like me playing with your nipples? Do you like when I'm a bit rough with them?"

"*Yesss,*" Skyler hisses. "More. Please. Please touch me more."

"Of course, I'm going to touch you more," Trevor assures him. "How could I not? You're so sexy for me. You know I can't resist you."

"You too," Skyler says. "So sexy."

"Thanks, baby. Are you wearing any underwear?"

He has to ask this, because Skyler either sleeps naked or in the tiniest little briefs known to man, depending on his mood.

"Yeah. Can I take them off?"

"Yes, I want you to take them off for me," Trevor tells him. "But remember, I'm the one who's doing it, right? And I'm going to run my hands down your sides first, then squeeze your hips before I start to peel those sexy briefs off you.

"*Mmm.*"

Trevor's starting to get hard from the idea of Skyler in bed, following all his instructions and getting turned on by it. But even if this game has woken Trevor up mentally, his body is still exhausted, so he's not sure if he'll be able to come. And that's totally fine. This is about Skyler, about making him feel good and less lonely.

"Are they off?" he asks.

"Yeah," Skyler says, and Trevor hears the shuffling of the covers as Skyler is likely trying to kick his underwear away. "What now?"

"Now that I can see your perfect, hard cock straining for me, I'm going to need to touch it, aren't I? I'm going to wrap my hand around your cock and give it a light squeeze before I stroke it up and down a few times. Can you do that for me?"

The small noise Skyler makes is confirmation, so Trevor keeps talking.

"This time on the upstroke, I'll sweep my thumb over the head of your cock. Then I can use the precum that's gathered there to make the slide of my hand easier when I go back to stroking."

Skyler sucks in a sharp breath, and Trevor grins to himself.

"Use your other hand to squeeze your inner thigh for me," he instructs. "I know you love it when I touch you there."

"*Mmm*, love it," Skyler confirms.

"Don't stop stroking. But don't go too fast. I want to jerk you off nice and slow and make it last."

All he gets from Skyler is a whimper.

"Do you need more, baby?" he asks.

"Yes! Wanna come. Make me come."

"Not yet. I want to enjoy you some more first."

Skyler whimpers again pitifully.

"Are you still stroking nice and slow like I told you to?" Trevor asks him. When he gets a quick affirmation, he continues. "You can let go of your thigh now. Use that hand to play with your balls, roll them around in your palm a bit. Do you like that?"

"Yes," Skyler breathes out.

Trevor starts stroking himself now too. He's almost fully hard, but despite how much he's enjoying listening to the sounds his husband makes, he still doesn't think he'll be able to get there. So he's not jerking off with the intention of coming. He only wants to take a little bit of the edge off, to feel good while he makes Skyler feel even better.

"Okay, baby," he says. "I need you to get the lube out of the bedside table now." From what he recalls of their last time at the apartment together, they still have a bottle there and it should still be good to use.

"I got it," Skyler says, anticipation seeping through in his voice.

As he lazily plays with his own balls, Trevor tells him, "Pour a tiny bit out on your fingers and rub them to warm it up. Then bring your hand down to your pretty hole for me, okay? Rub one finger around it first. Gently. Gotta get that hole ready."

"I'm ready, I'm ready," Skyler insists.

Trevor laughs softly. "Okay, I believe you. Slide one finger in. Just one finger, and don't go too deep."

"Oh my god, you're torturing me," Skyler whines.

"Am I?"

Skyler huffs and says, "You're mean." But Trevor's sure he's still following instructions like the good boy he loves to be. That is, of course, when he's not having fun being a total devil.

"God, you feel so good around my finger, baby," Trevor says, tugging lightly on his balls. "Your greedy hole wants to suck me in. But you can't, okay? Just play with that hole for me. We just wanna keep something inside you so you don't feel empty while I stroke your hard cock, right?"

There's a tiny whimper, and then a breathless, "*Trev?*"

"Yeah, baby?"

"I'm close."

"Are you ready to come?"

"Yes! Yes. Please make me come."

Trevor grins. "Well, since you said please so nicely. I'm gonna grip you harder now, jerk you faster, make sure I nudge that sensitive spot behind the head with every upstroke until you come for me. Go on. You deserve it, baby."

While he listens to the sounds of Skyler getting himself off, Trevor tucks his own cock away. The way Skyler moans out his name as he comes is more than enough satisfaction for him.

And as he waits for Skyler to come back down from his release, he imagines him there in bed, sloppily cleaning himself off, or maybe not even bothering, before he pulls the covers back up and rolls over onto his side. He'll probably instinctually reach for Trevor, even though Trevor's not there. But hopefully now, he'll at least be sated and relaxed enough to fall asleep alone.

"So good," Skyler finally whispers, sounding truly worn out. As he should be, after the events of his very long day. "Love you."

"I love you too, baby," Trevor tells him. "You should get some sleep now, okay?"

"Yeah, I'm so tired. Thank you."

"You don't need to thank me. I wish I could do more for you."

"I still wish you were here," Skyler admits. "But this was fun. Goodnight."

Trevor says goodnight, but after he hangs up, it takes him longer than it should to fall back asleep. Because damn. He really wishes he were there too.

SKYLER

ONE THING SKYLER ALWAYS TRIES to do if he's in New York for more than a night—besides see his sister, obviously—is visit his friend Betty. She lives in the same building, a couple floors below his penthouse, and she dotes on him like a grandmother. An eccentric grandmother who swears a lot and reads the filthiest smut, usually with knots or tentacles involved.

Skyler's pretty shameless about sex, and he and Trevor have often been accused of fucking like bunnies. But Betty once described a sex scene to him involving a guy *wearing* a bunny suit that made even him blush.

When she's not at home with her monster romance novels, Betty's out on the streets protesting for equality or gun reform. So she's pretty much the coolest septuagenarian he knows.

He met her early on when he moved into the building. They were in the elevator together, and when he tried to help her with her armload of grocery bags, she shook her head and said, "Back on up, scrawny. I might be old, but I'm not incapable."

He's so used to helping out anyone whenever he can that he didn't know what to do with himself at the rejection. But then she laughed, told him he looked too skinny, and asked if he wanted to stop in at her place so she could make him some soup. She assumed that, because he was a guy in his twenties, he didn't know how to feed himself. And she still always has food ready for him whenever he comes over. He's never had the heart to tell her that he actually loves to cook.

Knocking on her door in the late afternoon now, Skyler's already prepared for trying to convince her he's too full from his lunch to eat anything. The door flies open only a few seconds later, and she beams as soon as she sees him, yanking him in for a hug. The strength in her tiny arms would be surprising if he wasn't used to it.

"Hi, gorgeous," she says. "It's good to see you."

"You too. You look good," he tells her, pulling away to actually get a better look at her.

Her thinning, chin-length hair is dyed light pink, a different color than it was the last time he was here. She once explained that she'd been a brunette all her life, so when her hair turned gray, she decided that if she was going to dye it, she might as well dye it a fun color instead of the same old boring brown.

She's wearing a purple T-shirt that says HOES BEFORE BROS and jeans that hang loosely off her small, thin frame. Skyler doesn't like how she appears to have shrunk a bit more or gotten frailer every time he sees her. But her energy level always remains high, and she never seems to have any trouble getting around, so hopefully her health is still holding strong.

She tuts, ushering him inside. "I look old. You can say it. But don't worry. I'm not dying yet."

He almost laughs but not quite. Following her into the kitchen, he obediently takes a seat at the small table when she forcefully pushes him down into it.

"I've still got too much shit to try to fix in this damn country," she says as she moves over to the stove. "Everything's falling apart again. New horrible crap going on every day. It's ridiculous. Like these assholes have never read a history book or something. And now I'm out here making even more protest signs than I ever did back in my twenties. Why can't they just treat everyone the same and let folks go on living their own lives as long as they're not hurting anybody?"

Skyler sighs. "I wish it could be that way."

"It can," Betty states firmly. "But the people with the most power and money are always greedy for more of it. And they trick the people without any of that stuff into believing that their own neighbors who look a bit different than them are to blame for their lives being hard. Rather than blaming the dicks who control everything."

While Skyler totally agrees with her, he also feels a tinge of guilt. Because even though he's always done what he can to make this world a better place for everyone, he *is* one of those people with way more money than he'll ever need. And even though his level of fame puts him under constant public scrutiny, his fame and money have certainly kept him well-insulated from the worst of this country's issues.

"Oh, don't make that face," Betty says, shaking her head at him before opening the oven. She bends down and pulls a square pan out of it. "I know you're rich as all fuck, but that doesn't make you one of those assholes I'm talking about. You've got the biggest heart of anyone I've ever met. And you use your money and influence for good, same as me."

Skyler knows Betty was married a long time ago to a bank CEO. But they apparently caused a large scandal when it came out that they were living as a triad with another woman. And the woman was a pretty famous artist in the New York art scene back at that time. So Betty's always been a proponent for what some other people might consider unconventional lifestyles.

Both of her partners died sooner than they should have, though. Which means she's been alone for a long time, with a lot of money and looking for ways to fill her time.

He accepts a plate with a large piece of cherry cobbler dished onto it that she passes to him. He didn't have a chance to tell her he wasn't hungry. Not that she would've listened anyway. When she takes the seat across from him, setting down a plate with a much smaller piece of cobbler for herself, their conversation drifts to happier topics. Like smut.

Betty's more than happy to talk about her current read when Skyler prompts her. "The guy's a dark angel, and you won't believe what he can do to the woman with his wings. Have you watched that show *Lucifer*?"

Skyler suppresses a laugh as he takes a tiny bite of dessert. He's never seen the show, but he's pretty sure that whatever she's about to describe to him isn't in it.

After she's told him much more than he needed to know about angel sex, Betty jumps up from the table asking, "Do you want some tea?"

She's already grabbed the electric kettle before he can answer, so he lets her make it. She sets the tea down in front of him in a mug with a picture of a uterus holding up two middle fingers.

While he waits for the tea to cool down a bit, Skyler thanks her for taking care of his plants. Ever since he bought a bunch of succulents on that trip with Trevor during the wildfire, he's wanted to keep more plants in the apartment, so that the place actually feels alive whenever he visits. But he's not here nearly enough, and they'd die without someone's help.

He would've had Layla do it, except he doesn't trust her not to kill them. Plants aren't her thing. She can keep multiple patients alive each day, so you might think she could handle a cactus, but you'd be wrong.

Skyler was reluctant to accept Betty's help, but she'd insisted. And she'd absolutely refused to let him pay her for doing it.

"So where's your other half?" Betty asks him. "Is he not with you?"

That makes Skyler frown. The phone sex with Trevor last night was hot, but he still misses him. And he knows that's ridiculous. They're married. They live together. It won't kill him to spend a few nights away from his husband.

He's just greedy. He went too long without having Trevor by his side, and he never wants to go through life like that again.

Betty raises an eyebrow, and he realizes he hasn't answered.

"No, Trev couldn't come. He's been super busy with his new label. It's going really well."

"That's great, isn't it? So why do you not look happy about it?"

"I am!" Skyler exclaims. Because of course, he is. He'll always be happy about Trevor's success. What kind of shitty partner would he be if he wasn't? "I'm just being silly."

Wrapping her bony fingers around the handle of her mug, Betty says slowly, "Your feelings are never silly. You're allowed to feel however you feel."

Skyler shakes his head. "No, but I really am happy for him. And I'm so freaking proud. I'm glad he found his passion in the music industry again. And he's doing fantastic. He already signed this artist who's incredible, and I think the guy's gonna go so far. I honestly don't expect Trevor to spend every waking minute with me. Sometimes I get anxious, that's all."

He pauses, taking a sip of tea to gather his thoughts before he speaks again. "Our lives were so crazy when we were in the band together. And eventually, all the different obligations took a toll on our relationship."

Betty gives him a skeptical look. "Didn't they have you two pretending to date a bunch of girls, though? You've told me that was what caused the problems."

"Yeah. It was the biggest factor. So I know it's different now, but still. I don't want our busy careers to keep us from actually being together. Living our lives together. But I'm not ready to quit music, and I'd never want him to give up his career either. Like I said, sometimes I just get anxious thinking about it. The next time I go on tour, he probably won't be able to come with me for the whole thing, so what then? We spend a year apart? I hate that."

"I've only seen the two of you together a couple times now," Betty says, reaching out to place a hand on his forearm, "but it's impossible not to see how much you love each other. From what you've told me, I know you've been through a lot together, and you've been through a lot apart. When you decided to get back together, you were both in places in your lives where you understood the effort it would take to make it work, didn't you? You knew what your lives would be like, and you chose it."

"We did." Skyler manages a smile. "And I know every relationship takes effort. Believe me, I'm not complaining about that. Actually, it took more effort to be away from Trevor for all that time than it does to be with him. Being with him is the best part. It makes everything else worth it. I'll try to remember that whenever I'm sad about us being apart for a bit." His smile grows bigger now when he adds, "At least I'll always get to go back to him."

"Damn straight," Betty says. She gives his arm a squeeze before letting it go. "Or maybe damn gay is more appropriate here."

That makes Skyler snort a laugh. "Thanks for this. I guess I needed to put things into perspective."

Betty lifts one leg to put her foot up on the edge of her seat, which is a pretty impressive display of flexibility for someone her age. "When we first met after you moved in here, you were devastated over your breakup. I know how lost you felt. But I also remember you slowly putting yourself back together. You learned how to build your own life without Trevor. You're one of the most interesting people I've ever met, and I'm old, so you know I've met plenty of people."

"What are you trying to say?"

"I'm saying that you have a shit ton of interests and hobbies of your own. Not to mention, your ridiculously huge career. You might be the world's best husband or something. But that's not all you are. You have your own life outside of Trevor." Betty stares him down hard, like she wants to make sure he's paying attention. "You don't stop being a person when he's not around, do you? I'm sure the two of you will be madly in love with each other every day for the rest of your lives, but you don't need to be together every damn day for that to be true."

Well, shit.

Skyler already knew all of this. Really, he did. But hearing someone else say it to him is a pretty good reminder.

Sun & Star Records is only going to grow bigger, and it will take up even more of Trevor's time than it does now. And eventually, Skyler's going to tour again. He's not going to hold himself back, and he would never want Trevor to do that either.

They loved each other even through the five years when they never spoke. They can be apart, go wherever they need to go on their own, and enjoy it. Their love isn't going anywhere.

When Skyler steps out of the elevator and back into the penthouse, he's armed with a plastic-wrapped plate of cobbler that Betty insisted he take. As he turns toward the open kitchen area to set it down on the breakfast bar, he gets a weird sense that something isn't right.

The TV is on.

Did he leave it on?

There's no way. He hasn't even watched TV since he's been here.

"Hey, baby." Trevor's head pops up over the back of the couch, and Skyler jumps out of his skin.

The shock only lasts a second, though, before he's running over to stand behind the couch. "Oh my god! What? Hi! How are you here?"

Shrugging casually like this is nothing, Trevor says, "Moved some things around. I rescheduled one meeting and figured Noah could handle the rest in my place. He was more than happy to jump in."

"But . . ." Skyler's elation at seeing Trevor starts to fade into a feeling of guilt. "You didn't need to do that for me. I know I whined a lot, but I was fine."

"I know you were." Trevor reaches up to grasp Skyler's wrist. "But I missed you. Hope you still want me here."

"Are you kidding?" Skyler says, launching himself over the back of the couch and practically tackling him.

After a hello kiss that lasts long enough for the closing credits music to play on the episode of *Gilmore Girls* Trevor was watching, Skyler gets up to grab a book off one of his shelves, and then they resettle on the couch together. Trevor's head is in Skyler's lap, and Skyler holds his book in one hand so he can keep the other one in Trevor's hair while Trevor watches another episode.

And this, right here, is Skyler's idea of a perfect night. No performances, no partying. Just the two of them.

He may not *need* Trevor with him everywhere he goes. But he'll always want him there.

SEPTEMBER

SKYLER JAMES DISCUSSES THE POSSIBILTY OF HAVING CHILDREN WITH HUSBAND TREVOR BLUE

TREVOR

TREVOR HAD A LONG DAY AT WORK looking over contract negotiations, so when he arrives home, all he wants to do is relax his brain and hopefully eat something good Skyler made for dinner. Not that he *expects* Skyler to make dinner. But Skyler cooks for him more often than not, and you certainly won't find him complaining about it.

As he steps past the foyer and into the main living room, though, it's immediately clear that something isn't normal here. First of all, the house is noisy. Much more so than it would be if Skyler were here alone. And more than that, the place is a wreck. It looks like a tornado blew through the room. There are end tables stacked on top of each other, other furniture out of place and draped with sheets and blankets, and even more bedding spread out haphazardly on the floor.

Trevor eyes Stella, who thankfully seems unharmed. She's lying on top of a chair that's half-covered by a blanket and giving him a look that says, *I didn't do it.*

He believes her. She's too lazy to create this much of a mess.

Right as Trevor's about to call out for Skyler, his husband comes barreling around the corner with his watermelon-patterned beach towel tied around his neck and billowing behind him like a cape.

"Run!" Skyler shouts when he sees Trevor standing there. "They're after me!"

Despite the absurdity of the scene, Trevor has a moment of actual panic, his eyes scanning the room for the threat, body ready to launch into action. Then two child-sized figures in gorilla masks appear, stumbling over their own feet in their pursuit.

Skyler darts behind Trevor, gripping Trevor's forearms to keep him in place. "You have to protect me! I don't want to get eaten!"

All Trevor can do as the tiny gorillas head right for him is let out a short laugh and a confused, "Um."

"Never mind," Skyler says, letting go of Trevor and dashing away. "Save yourself! I can outrun them!"

The gorillas bypass Trevor and chase Skyler back out of the room. A few moments later, there's a crashing sound, followed by loud squeals of laughter.

Since it doesn't sound like anyone's hurt, Trevor stays where he is, surveying the messy room some more. There's a very tacky looking golden box lying open on the floor in front of one of the couches. It appears to be filled with jewelry, and after stepping closer and bending down to see, Trevor recognizes that most of it is Skyler's jewelry. Although that's certainly not one of Skyler's jewelry boxes.

"That's our treasure!" a small voice exclaims.

Trevor looks up to find both of Annie's kids coming over, sans-masks, with Skyler right on their heels, looking winded but grinning.

"We had a treasure hunt," Skyler explains.

"Uh huh." Trevor glances again at the jewelry. Not all of Skyler's jewelry is expensive, but some of it definitely is. But he's not too surprised that Skyler isn't worried about any of it breaking or going missing.

Skyler gathers up the couple of blankets that were strewn across the couch and tosses them to the floor before sitting down. The kids immediately throw themselves on the floor and start rolling around in the bedding. Trevor carefully sidesteps them to sit beside Skyler.

"Annie needed Mike to babysit," Skyler says. "But I was bored, so I asked if I could do it."

"Uh huh," Trevor says again, amused.

But Skyler must not pick up on the amusement, because he winces. "I know we made a mess. Don't worry, I'll clean everything up."

Setting a hand on Skyler's thigh, Trevor assures him, "I'm not mad. I'm only trying to figure out what the heck happened here."

"We were trying to build the world's most epic fort. But apparently, I'm not the best structural engineer."

"Well, I guess you can't be great at everything, can you?" Trevor says, giving Skyler a quick kiss on the cheek. "That wouldn't be fair."

Skyler places his hand over Trevor's and threads their fingers together.

Glancing down, Trevor notices the opal ring—the one he originally had engraved for Skyler what feels like a lifetime ago—is on Skyler's finger. Not in the treasure chest.

That ring means a lot to both of them.

"I'm sorry I don't have anything started for dinner," Skyler says. "I sent Mike out to the store to grab a bag of chicken nuggets for the kids, and I have some sweet potatoes in the pantry, so I was going to make them sweet potato fries to go with the nuggets. But I haven't had time to think of what to make for us."

"Baby, you don't have to apologize to me for that," Trevor tells him. "The only reason I don't do more of the cooking for us is because I know you love doing it. But you never *have* to cook for me."

"I know."

One of the kids knocks into Trevor's leg like a little wrecking ball. It startles him, but then he smiles at his husband. "Besides, I'm cool with nuggets and fries for dinner."

For a few seconds, Skyler just looks at him, his green eyes lit up with happiness. Trevor kind of wishes the kids weren't here so he could kiss him. Well, maybe more than kiss him. Maybe kiss the parts of him that would be totally unacceptable to kiss in front of the kids.

But it's okay, because he can see how much fun Skyler's having babysitting. And this is certainly an interesting change to their normal evening routine, but Trevor is finding that he doesn't mind it at all.

He could see this for them. In the future. He doesn't know how far off that future might need to be, but he can see it.

While Skyler gets the oven preheated and the sweet potatoes sliced up, Trevor helps the kids make their fort a bit more epic. They're easily impressed by his building skills, but he's not entirely sure how to entertain them once they've all gotten inside the fort, so he's glad when Skyler returns and crawls in with them. The kids gravitate toward him, and Trevor participates in the game Skyler makes up, but mostly he sits there and watches his husband.

It seems he'll never stop being awed by Skyler. By his playfulness, joy, and creativity. And by the endless amount of love he has to give.

When they were in New York last month, Skyler did that interview for a morning show. The primary focus was supposed to be his role in the upcoming Disney movie, but with Skyler talking about how important it is to include queer representtation in children's media, that led the hosts into asking him very personal questions about he and Trevor's relationship and whether they were planning to start their own family.

Skyler was vague about it at first, only admitting that he'd love to have children someday, while telling them he wasn't sure if or when it would be possible. But as Trevor sat in the greenroom watching on a monitor, he could see it so clearly—how *deeply* Skyler wants this.

The hosts continued to pry, asking which avenue Skyler and Trevor would pursue if they did decide to have children, and how it might affect their careers. Skyler, being Skyler, remained nothing but pleasant as he tried his best to give answers. But the truth was, he obviously didn't have all the answers. And neither did Trevor.

These were all the questions that had already been running through Trevor's mind leading up to this interview, and hearing Skyler talk about the subject only confirmed for Trevor that Skyler has been thinking about all this too.

Of course, the other thing the interview did was bring about a whole slew of gossip articles speculating on the subject. Speculating on Trevor and Skyler's very private lives. But they're used to that.

He and Skyler have always been able to talk about anything. And since they came back into each other's lives after the breakup, they've only gotten even better at communicating. So Trevor's honestly not sure why he hasn't brought up the topic of children with Skyler yet. He's been dealing with a lot of work stuff, sure, but that's not a good enough reason not to have time to talk to his husband.

When dinner is ready, both kids want Skyler to carry them into the dining room, and for a second, they start arguing about it. But Skyler is quick to solve this problem. He crouches down so one kid can jump on his back, then scoops the other up in his arms, and everyone's happy.

As Trevor follows behind the three of them, he can't get over how perfect that picture is. It's something he could love seeing every day. So he decides right now that he's going to make time for this conversation as soon as possible.

SKYLER

WHEN TREVOR ASKED SKYLER if he wanted to go out for dinner at Skyler's favorite Japanese restaurant, Skyler naturally said yes. They rarely come here, for a couple of reasons. The first being that this is a tiny family-owned business, so it can't offer the same level of privacy and security that they would get at one of the more high-end or private club restaurants. If they want to eat here, they need to pay out the restaurant to close early for them.

While the money's not an issue, Skyler doesn't particularly like doing this. It makes him feel grossly entitled. But the older couple that owns the restaurant are always more than happy to accommodate them—because they're obviously compensated very well for their trouble. And they do their best to treat Skyler and Trevor like regular customers, despite the fact that they're sitting here in a place that was closed down just for them.

The other reason they don't often eat here is because Japanese cuisine isn't Trevor's favorite. He loves sushi rolls and will eat some sashimi, but he doesn't care for all the variety of other authentic dishes that Skyler loves to get here.

At first, Skyler didn't think it was too out of the ordinary, though, when Trevor suggested they come here. Trevor always goes out of his way to make Skyler happy for no particular reason at all. But now, as Skyler picks through his seaweed salad with his chopsticks and Trevor doesn't do much to initiate a conversation, Skyler is starting to get nervous.

Mike and Hal are both here with them, but while they'd normally eat with them or at a table across the room, tonight Trevor asked if they wouldn't mind eating in the back staff area to give him and Skyler more privacy. And although the guys didn't seem at all bothered by the request, Skyler is wondering why Trevor wanted that.

Mike and Hal are practically family.

It makes him think there's something serious going on that Trevor wants to talk about, but he can't imagine what it could be. And so far, Trevor's only made small talk about work.

"Is something wrong?" Skyler finally asks. Because this is stupid. He shouldn't be nervous around his freaking husband. Trevor makes him feel more comfortable than anyone else he's ever known. When he's not acting strange, that is.

Trevor frowns. "No, of course not. Why would you think that?"

"I dunno," Skyler says, then gestures at the empty room around them. "Something feels off about this."

"I'm sorry." Reaching across the small table, Trevor rubs his thumb over the back of Skyler's hand. "I wanted us to have a nice night together. We haven't gotten to go out like this in a while."

Skyler melts a little. It's crazy how, after so many years together and all the cool things they've gotten to do, a sentiment as simple as that can still make him feel all gooey inside.

"There was something I wanted to talk to you about though."

Well, fuck.

Before he responds, Skyler sets down his chopsticks and flips his hand over to take Trevor's. He *knew* something was going on. "What is it?"

Trevor squeezes his hand reassuringly. "Nothing bad, I swear. I've just been thinking about this a lot lately. Not sure why I didn't say anything sooner, honestly, but I was wondering . . ."

In the long pause, Skyler slides his hand free and grabs his chopsticks to take another bite of his salad, even though he's suddenly not very hungry. Then, unable to stand Trevor's hesitation any longer, he says, "Just tell me, please. You're making me nervous."

"Well," Trevor tries again. "Since we got married, we haven't discussed any plans for having kids. It was something we both said we really wanted back when we were still practically kids ourselves. But I'd like to know where your head's at with the idea now."

Oh, shit. This is because of that stupid interview last month. Skyler was talking about the importance of queer representation in children's media, so of course the hosts asked him if he planned to have children of his own. And he wasn't going to lie. He's always wanted that. But he needed to be diplomatic in his answer to try to avoid getting the rumor mill churning. So he said that, while he wants it, he isn't sure if having a family would be possible for him and Trevor with the way their lives are.

All the celebrity gossip sites latched on to his words anyway and spun them off in all different directions. Some articles falsely claimed that he and Trevor were spotted visiting adoption agencies and surrogacy clinics, while others speculated that he and Trevor wanted different things and it was causing issues between them.

And while they've accepted the fact that there will always be people talking about their relationship now that they've made it public, Skyler knows it still sometimes bothers Trevor when people try to dig into the really personal stuff. So he can't blame Trevor for being upset that he accidentally sparked all these articles.

"Baby."

His eyes shoot up from his tiny bowl to see Trevor watching him, concern that Skyler can't really make sense of etched into his face.

"I'm sorry," Skyler says, since that seems like a good place to start.

Trevor's brow furrows. "Why are you apologizing?"

"Um. I know I could've refused to answer that question in my interview. I shouldn't have said anything. I should have known everyone else would start talking about it, and that you wouldn't . . ." Skyler takes a breath, trying to ease his anxiety as he presses his thumb over the tiny flower engraved on his saki glass. "I wasn't trying to force you into having kids with me."

"Baby, what are you even talking about?" Trevor says. "I'm not mad about your interview. You didn't do anything wrong."

Oh. Well, yeah. Logically, Skyler knew that.

But then why does he feel guilty about it?

He's not really sure. He's just sort of come to accept over the years that his dream of having a big family has become increasingly more unlikely the higher his level of fame has soared. His lifestyle—touring all the time, needing a bodyguard practically every time he leaves his house—isn't exactly conducive to raising children.

"I didn't want you to think it was something I expected," he tells Trevor. "I know it would be too much."

"Why do you think it would be too much?" Trevor asks.

Skyler scoffs. "Come on. I'm not crazy."

"Have I ever said you were?" Trevor's tone is unfailingly patient, even as Skyler starts to feel petulant.

He tends to get this way whenever he really wants something that he knows he can't have. And sometimes it's easier to pretend he doesn't want something, rather than admit that he does.

"How would we be able to have kids when we're both so damn busy?" he asks, raising his voice a bit too loudly for the empty restaurant. Hopefully, the staff is too occupied in the back to hear him. "You want me to have kids living in my home while I barely know them because I spend half my life flying all over the world?"

"Okay, hold on," Trevor says calmly. "We don't need to figure out all the details of how we'd make it work right now. I'm only asking if having kids is still something you want."

"Well, it's a stupid thing to ask."

As soon as he says this, Skyler cringes. *Fuck.* He's being mean now, and he doesn't want to be. Trevor did nothing to deserve him acting this way. Trevor did a sweet thing for him, making plans to have this restaurant shut down so he could bring Skyler here and they could have a nice night out together. All because he knows Skyler loves this place.

Now, Trevor's silence is loud, and Skyler glances upward, rather than face the disappointed look his husband must be giving him. There are strings of cherry blossoms hanging from the ceiling. They must be fake, but they're still beautiful.

This restaurant is too pretty of a place to be fighting in.

Before Skyler can apologize for his immature remark, though, Mrs. Nakamura, one of the owners, appears from the back, carrying their entrees. Skyler thanks her sincerely when she sets down his grilled octopus dish, and Trevor kindly assures her that they don't need anything else after she places his ramen in front of him.

But the look Trevor gives him after the woman disappears makes Skyler squirm like his dinner probably did before it was caught. He glances down at the dish and realizes he's pretty much lost all his appetite now. Which is a shame, because this poor creature shouldn't have died for nothing.

He might need to look into becoming a vegan.

"I guess we should've had this conversation at home," Trevor says, aggressively snatching up some noodles between his chopsticks. "I didn't realize it would upset you."

Skyler's more embarrassed than upset now, but he doesn't disagree when

Trevor suggests they drop the subject for the time being and enjoy their dinners.

He doesn't really enjoy his dinner, though. His meal is incredible—the food here always is. But he knows Trevor will want to keep talking about this at home. So even while he engages with Trevor in a conversation about a feature Skyler agreed to do for a song on a friend's new album, he's trying to figure out how he'll convince Trevor that he's not upset about them not having kids.

Trevor already gives him everything. Skyler doesn't need more.

He doesn't.

It's fine if he never gets to be a father.

THE DRIVE HOME ONLY TOOK THIRTY-FIVE MINUTES, but it felt a lot longer considering the tension in the backseat. Although Skyler and Trevor normally talk and behave freely around Mike and Hal, there are some things they don't subject the security guys to. Like sex (intentionally, at least) and fighting.

So Trevor spent most of the ride leaning forward to talk to the guys about some sports thing Skyler didn't understand. He barely acknowledged Skyler, which made Skyler feel so itchy in his skin that he had to fight the urge to scratch it all off. But Skyler can't blame him, because Trevor knows Skyler well enough to gauge his moods, and ignoring him was probably the safest thing to do.

In the car, Skyler wasn't anywhere near ready to have the rational conversation Trevor's looking for. He's still not ready, honestly, but he loves his husband more than anything. The last thing he wants to do is fight with him, so they need to talk this out like adults.

He knows the conversation is coming as Trevor silently follows him upstairs and into their bedroom. To stall a minute longer, Skyler goes into their closet to change out of his clothes. He puts on a lightweight pair of sleep shorts and nothing else. His skin still feels kind of itchy.

When he comes back out, Trevor is sitting on the edge of the bed. His shoes are off and his button-up removed, but he's still dressed in his slacks and black undershirt. Trevor pats the bed beside him, and Skyler obediently goes over, feeling a little bit like he's being led to an execution.

God, he's dramatic.

He climbs on and sits cross-legged—because if he perches on the edge, it'll be easier to bolt if he doesn't like where this conversation goes. And he doesn't want to do that. No drama.

He's not a teenager anymore. He's more mature, and he and Trevor agreed they wouldn't run from any problems they might have. Running from problems means running from each other, and Skyler will never run from Trevor again.

Although, he wishes they could simply ignore the problem and hope it goes away, rather than get it out in the open where they have to admit to it. So maybe he's not that mature.

Angling his body Skyler's way, Trevor asks him, "Can you please explain what's happening here? Let me in on what's going through that gorgeous head of yours."

Skyler focuses down on his legs, at the lion tattooed on his thigh. For a moment, he imagines it coming to life and swallowing him whole so that he doesn't have to dissect what he's feeling. Because he's pretty sure that what's going through his head is fear. That's what this comes down to.

His worst fear is losing Trevor, despite how much he believes that will never happen. He knows they made vows. *'Til death do us part,* and all that. And he doesn't even need any vows to know how much they love each other. But still. He lost him once before, and even if it was only temporary, he never wants to experience that kind of devastation again. So at the end of the day, yeah, it's his worst fear.

And that's why he was so touchy at dinner about the topic of having children. He doesn't want to admit how much it hurts to think about it. About how he and Trevor will most likely never be able to start a family like they used to dream they would. Like Skyler's always wanted.

He doesn't want Trevor to think he's not enough for Skyler.

He fucking is.

He's everything to him.

Trevor is his sun. Without him, there's no warmth.

"Hey," Trevor says gently. And when Skyler reluctantly looks at him, he carefully tucks some of Skyler's hair behind his ear. "It's okay. It doesn't matter what you said in that interview or what any stupid article says about us. If you don't want kids—"

"Of course, I want kids!" Skyler blurts out. Because he's tried to skirt around the subject tonight, but he can't keep the truth in forever. He can't keep it from the man he loves. "I've wanted to have kids with you since I was nineteen. But back then, we couldn't have grasped how famous we'd become. So I just don't see how it would be possible now. Plus I wasn't sure if it was something you still wanted after . . . after everything."

After Trevor's ex-wife let him believe they'd lost a baby when she was never pregnant at all, for starters. He knows how much that messed Trevor up.

"You should've asked me about it," Trevor says. And then quickly, he adds, "And, yes, I know that's unfair to say, because I should've asked you about this sooner, too."

"Why didn't you?"

Trevor cups Skyler's face with one hand, smoothing out Skyler's prickly edges. "It wasn't the first thing on my mind right after we got married," he says, his blue eyes shining with sincerity. "Because all I could think about then was how lucky I am that I'll get to spend the rest of my life with you."

"*Oh.*" Skyler's response is practically a whisper. If his voice was working properly, he'd tell Trevor how Skyler's the lucky one. Being loved by Trevor—even when Skyler's acting like a fool—is an incredible gift that Skyler tries to never take for granted.

"But my feelings on having kids haven't changed." Trevor runs his thumb softly along Skyler's cheekbone, and Skyler leans his face into the touch like a cat. "You know it's always been something I've wanted. And having them with *you* . . . that's something I want very much if you do too."

Skyler struggles for what to say. There's still a part of him afraid to admit the truth, because he doesn't want to set himself up for disappointment, and he doesn't want his husband to ever feel like less than everything he needs. But it's hard to hide his feelings when Trevor's looking at him like this. And hiding his feelings from the person he trusts most in the world is stupid anyway.

So finally, he just says, "Well, I do."

Trevor smiles, dropping his hand from Skyler's face only to trail his fingertips along Skyler's thigh instead. "So we're saying we both want the same thing?"

"Yeah, I guess so."

"Then why are we fighting?"

Skyler frowns. He doesn't think tonight reached full fight status, but his stubbornness and defensiveness surely could've taken it there. Thankfully, though, Trevor can break down all his silly defenses like they're nothing.

Somehow this man makes Skyler happy to be defenseless.

They're both unarmed inside this house. In this room, on this bed. Together, face to face. Here they're not Skyler James and Trevor Blue, the public personas that the rest of the world sees. With each other, they're everything and nothing more than who they are.

Skyler has nothing to hide here.

"I don't know," he admits, shifting closer in a way that encourages Trevor's fingers to trail higher, because Trevor's touch will always give him comfort. "I don't know why I acted like I did tonight. Except maybe it's because I'm aware that I have this totally incredible life. I have everything I've ever wanted. More than I could've dreamed of, and yet, I still want one more thing. I feel greedy."

"You're not—" Trevor starts, but Skyler shakes his head to cut him off.

He needs to get this out.

"I don't want you to think I'm not satisfied with the life we have now. You are the most important thing in the world to me. And if it's just you and me forever, then I'll be so happy with that. Ever since I met you, you've been all I've needed. The only thing I love more than music is you. I don't need the global stardom, don't need this huge house. I don't need to have kids in order to be unbelievably fucking happy every day of my life. I only need you."

The waistband of his shorts suddenly tug at his hip, and Skyler glances down to find Trevor's fingers curled tightly into the bottom of them. When he looks back up, the burning intensity in Trevor's eyes makes him suck in a breath.

"Baby, you know I feel the same, right?" Trevor says. "I love you more than anything else on this planet. And as long as I get to spend the rest of my life with you, then I'll be the happiest man on Earth." He skims his hand up underneath Skyler's shorts and squeezes the outside of his thigh. "But you're allowed to want other things too. It's okay that you want kids, and it's okay that when we have them, you'll love the shit out of them. It won't mean you love me any less. And it doesn't make you greedy at all, either. It makes you someone who has so much damn love to give, and it's going to make any kids we have lucky as hell."

Oh god. How does this perfect man always know exactly the right things to say to make any doubts in Skyler's head go quiet?

He practically launches himself at his husband. In his haste to climb into Trevor's lap, he knocks him onto his back. But it's okay, because this is also a very acceptable position. Yup. No objections.

"I fucking love you," he says, grinning uncontrollably.

Trevor's hands clutch his naked waist. "I love you too. You're my stars."

"You're my sun," Skyler tells him. Then he leans down for a kiss, wanting the sun to consume him, to burn him up.

But to Skyler's dismay, Trevor only kisses him back for a couple seconds before he gets a grip on Skyler's head and gently urges him back, making a face.

"What?" Skyler asks.

"Your breath tastes like slimy octopus."

Skyler huffs in disbelief, because seriously? "You don't care when my breath tastes like your *ass*, but you draw the line at octopus?"

"It's slimy," Trevor repeats with a tone more serious than this moment deserves. And then he stares at Skyler, still holding him back, until Skyler rolls his eyes and relents.

"Fine. Lemme go brush my teeth." Hopping off the bed, he adds, "But I expect you to be waiting here naked for me when I'm finished."

After the quickest round of brushing he can manage, he returns from the bathroom and is very pleased to find that Trevor followed his instructions. Although his instructions didn't include for Trevor to be slowly stroking himself, but his husband has always been good about taking initiative. Skyler's a lucky man.

He hastily sheds his shorts, then climbs onto the bed. This time when he gets on top of Trevor, Trevor immediately pulls him down and licks right into Skyler's mouth.

"*Mmm*," Trevor moans against Skyler's lips as he slows down the kiss. "Much better."

Trevor's hands are everywhere now as they kiss, roaming Skyler's back, tangled in his hair, gripping his waist, grazing up and down his thighs. Their erections glide together as Trevor continues to explore every crevice of Skyler's mouth and Skyler writhes on top of him.

Finally, Trevor's hands land on Skyler's ass. He spreads Skyler's cheeks and holds them apart so his cock can slip in between them. Then he finds a rhythm, rocking his hips up while using his hold on Skyler's ass to guide Skyler up and down.

Skyler allows his husband the control for a minute, then he pulls his mouth from Trevor's and braces his hands on Trevor's chest as he takes over and starts to ride him like that. They're both breathing hard, Trevor muttering encouragements for

Skyler to keep it up.

Before long, things slow down, the sense of urgency fading into something softer. And that's when the full extent of what Trevor told Skyler truly sinks in. Not just the part about how much Trevor loves him, though that was nice. But that Trevor still wants to have kids with him, that he believes it's something they can actually make happen. That Skyler's dream could be a reality.

Skyler knows Trevor would sacrifice things to make him happy, but he doesn't want it to come to that. He won't let Trevor set his career aside in order for Skyler to keep his own *and* have a family. Hopefully, they can find a way where nobody has to sacrifice anything.

Trevor loosens his hold on Skyler's ass, sliding one hand all the way up his spine to hold the back of his neck. "What are you thinking about?"

Smiling, Skyler replies, "Just how you're so good to me."

"Baby," is all Trevor says. But that one word tells Skyler everything he needs to know.

Skyler is in a very happy place as he leans back down to plant kisses over Trevor's chest. He pays special attention to the tattoo above his left pec. The one of the cards that say ALL IN.

All fucking in.

Pointing his tongue, he traces along the edges of the tattoo while he uses his fingers to play with Trevor's nipple. Trevor's cock jerks against his ass, and Skyler grins smugly to himself. When he moves up to kiss and suck at Trevor's neck, Trevor moans and squeezes one of Skyler's ass cheeks hard, making Skyler gasp. And the lust quickly ramps back up from there.

As Skyler continues lavishing attention on Trevor's neck, Trevor sucks one finger into his mouth, then sneaks his hand between Skyler's cheeks and starts playing with his hole, rubbing his finger around the rim. Feeling the finger slowly pushing inside him, Skyler raises his head to peer down at Trevor. Without proper lube, even the one finger causes a slight burn as it stretches him, but his body adapts quickly.

This isn't the first and won't be the last time Trevor fingers his ass without proper lube. They'll need to stop and grab it at some point, once Skyler's desperate for more, but for right now, he's content with Trevor slowly fucking the one finger in and out of him. They stare at each other as Trevor does this, and the intimacy is overwhelming in the best way.

"Feel good, baby?" Trevor asks.

Even though the answer is obvious, Skyler nods a few times. "Yes. Good. Love it."

"I could just play with your tight little hole all night. I love watching your face as I make you feel good. But I also wanna taste you. Come up here and sit on my face."

Trevor pats Skyler's ass cheek with his free hand and Skyler jolts, spurring into action. Trevor's finger slips from his hole as Skyler scrambles up Trevor's body to get into position. And Skyler would mourn the loss of it if he didn't know that what's coming next will feel even better. He starts to lower himself cautiously over Trevor's face, but then Trevor yanks his ass down all the way, apparently unconcerned about getting smothered.

Skyler almost giggles at the thought of how Trevor was grossed out by Skyler eating octopus, but now he's diving his tongue into Skyler's hole, eating his ass ravenously like it's his favorite meal.

The tip of Skyler's cock smears precum on one of the pillows propped against the headboard as he wriggles around, unable to keep still while Trevor is working magic on him. He'll need to remember to toss that one on the floor before they go to sleep.

It's not long before Skyler's feeling delirious with pleasure. He needs Trevor to fuck him now while he still has control of his limbs. He lifts off Trevor's face, ignoring Trevor's noise of protest and the way he reaches for Skyler's ass to try to pull him back.

"I need you," Skyler tells him with a desperate edge in his voice. "Please. I'm ready."

Trevor nods and wipes at his mouth, letting Skyler move off him long enough to reach into the nightstand and grab the lube. Skyler slicks up Trevor's hard cock, more than ready to take it. Then he positions himself so he's straddling Trevor's hips again, and Trevor grabs his cock and helps Skyler line it up with his hole. As soon as the head presses against Skyler's rim, Trevor lets himself go and brings his hands to Skyler's hips to guide Skyler down onto him. Not that Skyler needs the help, but he appreciates how Trevor is always trying to take care of him.

Together, they move so Trevor's cock slides all the way into Skyler's hole in one steady motion. It's a lot all at once after only having one finger and Trevor's tongue inside him, and it takes Skyler's body a few seconds to adjust to the stretch. But then it's off to the races as Skyler eagerly begins to rock himself up and down his husband's perfect cock. Trevor lets him set the pace and then matches it, thrusting up every time Skyler grinds down.

God, Skyler loves this man with everything he has. He's loved him for so damn long, and he only loves him even more every single day. Because Trevor gives him more and more every day. Trevor already gives him everything, and now Trevor's going to find a way to give Skyler children.

"Oh yeah, right there," Skyler says breathlessly as Trevor's cock hits just the right spot inside him. "Are you gonna put a baby in me?"

Trevor eyes him almost cautiously but keeps fucking him. "Is this going to be a new kink for you?"

With a laugh, Skyler assures him, "No, sorry. I just couldn't help myself." Then he thinks about it for a second and asks, "But would you judge me if it was?"

"No, of course not," Trevor is quick to answer. "I'd never judge you for anything you want to try in bed. You should know that by now."

Skyler grins. "I do."

His husband never fails to make him feel safe and brave and understood. And he'll always love him for that. Among many, many other things.

But no, he's pretty sure he doesn't have a breeding kink.

They're quiet after that, each focused on both giving pleasure and taking it. They kiss and grope, eventually building up to a much faster pace until Skyler is riding Trevor for all he's worth. His thigh muscles will regret this in the morning, but the rest of him never will.

Then Trevor sharply smacks Skyler's ass cheek, and Skyler's hole clenches automatically around Trevor's cock while it's deep inside him.

"*Unngh*," Trevor groans loudly. "That's it. Go on and milk my cock, baby."

Skyler's eyes roll back, both at the words and at the way Trevor angles his hips to nail Skyler's prostate, lighting up a thousand different nerve endings and making him see stars. Trevor's mouth has certainly gotten filthier over the years. A wonderful result of the way they've lost every last shred of inhibition with each other.

"Are you ready for me to fill you up with my cum?" Trevor asks. "Maybe I should plug your hole when I'm done to keep every drop inside your ass all night. See if I can get you pregnant that way."

The shiver that runs up Skyler's entire body surprises him. Because *fuck*. Skyler may have been joking before, but Trevor makes it sound so hot. He knows Trevor's only teasing, though. Going along with the joke Skyler started.

Skyler loves how they can always be playful with each other. They can joke, and explore, and still fuck each other like their lives depend on it.

"God, I'm close," Skyler whines. "So close."

"Me too, baby," Trevor tells him, circling his fist over the head of Skyler's leaking cock and rubbing in a circle. "You gonna come with me?"

"*Yesss!*"

All it takes is one hard stroke of Trevor's hand and Skyler's cock is spilling his release. As he rides the wave of his orgasm, he feels Trevor's hips stutter to a stop, his cock buried deep inside Skyler's ass.

He almost wishes Trevor *would* plug him up. Just for fun. He has a nice small one with a pretty purple jewel on the end. But there's no way his legs will work if he tries to stand up to get it, and he's not letting Trevor leave this bed either.

After a few moments, Trevor gently urges Skyler up enough so that he can pull out. Skyler kisses him lazily until he regains enough strength to roll off him. Then he snuggles up against Trevor's side, slinging one leg possessively over his hip and resting his head on Trevor's chest. This is one of his absolute favorite places to be.

With Trevor softly stroking Skyler's hair, Skyler's mind drifts back to children, and he asks, "Are you going to get mad at me when I can't say no to our kids, and I make you be the bad cop?"

"Are you really planning to do that?"

He thinks about it for a second. "Well, no. Not really. But I have a feeling I'll be the pushover parent."

"You definitely will be," Trevor agrees with a quiet chuckle. "But I know you'll always want what's best for our kids, so I'm sure you'll learn how to say no when you need to."

"Oh," Skyler says, running a finger idly over Trevor's pec muscle. "Yeah. I didn't think of it like that."

Trevor lifts his head from the pillow and presses a sweet kiss to Skyler's forehead. "You're going to be the most amazing father."

"So are you," Skyler tells him. Because that's so obvious. Trevor can handle anything, and he'll make sure their kids always have everything they need. Not just physically, but emotionally too.

The idea of them really starting a family any time soon still seems next to impossible with their lives being the way they are. But Skyler knows Trevor wouldn't lie to him. If he says they're going to have it someday, then they will.

"It doesn't have to be right now, you know," Skyler says.

The small, confused noise Trevor makes probably means he was already drifting off to sleep.

"I know there's no rush for us having kids," Skyler clarifies for him. "I've just been assuming it was something that wasn't going to happen, and I've tried to accept that, but it was hard. Now that I know you still want it as much as I do, and you think we can make it work someday . . . I'm happy. Maybe in five years I'll decide I'm done singing, and you'll have a whole team of people working for you at your label, and then it will be the right time."

"Maybe," Trevor says, wrapping an arm firmly around Skyler's lower back. "Although I'm not sure you'll ever be done singing. But the right time might also sneak up on us. You never know. As long as we know what we want, I think we'll be ready for it whenever the time comes."

Yeah. Skyler likes the sound of that.

"And you know we're already a family, right?" Trevor asks.

"Huh?" Skyler tilts his head up to look at him.

"Me and you," Trevor says, rubbing a hand down his back. "We live together and love each other and take care of each other. We're a family, even if it's only the two of us."

Oh. Skyler's eyes suddenly feel a little wet. Of course they're already a family, with or without kids. And he would never want to diminish that.

"I know we are," he says, gazing lovingly into his husband's blue eyes. "We're perfect."

OCTOBER

SKYLER JAMES AND TREVOR BLUE SPOTTED ON ROMANTIC JAMAICAN VACATION

SKYLER

AS SOON AS THE CONCIERGE EXITS THEIR BUNGALOW, Skyler is on his husband, pushing his body up against Trevor's and sliding a hand around the back of Trevor's neck to bring their mouths together. They almost trip over one of the bags on the floor, but Trevor manages to navigate them around it.

Skyler seizes the opportunity to shove Trevor down into one of the oversized armchairs, because it looks really comfortable and they should probably try it out. He immediately settles himself in Trevor's lap, straddling his thighs, and yeah. *Plenty of room. Very comfy. Ten out of ten.*

Trevor grabs Skyler by the hips and squeezes him. "Baby, we have a whole week. Shouldn't we unpack our stuff and get settled in first?"

"I think I'm already settled pretty nicely right here," Skyler says with a grin. And to emphasize his point, he wiggles his ass a bit on Trevor's lap. Trevor's not hard yet, but that will be all too easy to remedy. Just a little more wiggling should do it . . .

"*Baby.*"

The commanding tone behind the pet name halts Skyler's movements and sends a sexy shiver down his spine. Trevor slides one hand up Skyler's back until it's between his shoulder blades, then presses down. Message received, Skyler happily leans in for a kiss.

Trevor cuts it off much too quickly for Skyler's liking, though, so Skyler juts out his lip to illustrate his displeasure. And when Trevor places his thumb there, Skyler darts out his tongue for a taste of Trevor's skin.

Smiling softly, Trevor moves his hand to cradle the side of Skyler's neck. "Weren't you complaining on the flight that you were hungry? But you didn't want to eat anything because you were saving your appetite for all the good food you knew would be here?"

Hmm. Good point.

"All right," Skyler concedes. "So you call the chef and ask him to deliver us something in thirty minutes. That's all the time I need for round one."

That makes Trevor chuckle. "Should I be concerned about my dick falling off before the end of this vacation?"

"Don't act like you don't want to fuck just as much as I do."

"Of course I do, baby," Trevor assures him. And to prove it, he grabs Skyler by the hips again and guides him back and forth a couple times over his lap until Skyler can feel Trevor's cock starting to harden. "But I want to do other things with you, too. I want to get that couple's massage we planned, and I want to relax on the beach with frozen cocktails. Go horseback riding along the water, maybe book a guide to take us snorkeling. I'll be too tired for all that if you start fucking my brains out on day one."

Skyler considers what he's saying but then shakes his head. "That's what coffee is for. And Jamaica's known for its coffee, right?"

Laughing again, Trevor just says, "I love you."

Which Skyler will take as his husband's enthusiastic consent.

He lifts his hips up enough to reach into Trevor's front pocket and get his phone out. Handing it to him, Skyler says, "Ask for a carafe of coffee and a large fruit and cheese plate with extra dragon fruit. Maybe some croissants."

"What about that Jamaican flatbread thing you like?" Trevor asks, pulling up the contact for the private chef they've been assigned. They've already done some planning with him for a few of the nicer dinners they'll have.

"Ooh, yes, bammy! And remember, thirty minutes. No sooner."

With an eye roll, Trevor makes the call. While he relays their requests, Skyler resumes grinding on his lap. When he leans down to suck on Trevor's neck, Trevor quickly winds a hand in his hair and tugs him back. Undeterred, Skyler just keeps grinding, and Trevor doesn't relinquish his hold, basically forcing Skyler to pull his own hair as he moves. But the tiny bites of pain only turn him on more.

After what feels like forever to Skyler, but was really less than a minute, Trevor hangs up and sets his phone on the table beside them. Then he uses both hands to grip Skyler's ass cheeks and pull him fully against Trevor's cock, holding him there as he takes Skyler's mouth in a hard kiss.

Thrilled to finally be getting what he wants, Skyler returns the kiss hungrily. His tongue seeks out Trevor's as his hands roam over Trevor's abs and chest. They're both fully hard now. Skyler's reluctant to get off Trevor's lap, but his cock is begging to be freed from his pants. So he stands up and makes quick work of getting naked, pleased when he sees Trevor doing the same from his position in the chair.

"Lube?" Trevor asks.

Skyler nods, crouching down to unzip one of the side compartments of his duffle. He knows exactly where he put it. With the lube in hand, he takes his favorite seat back in Trevor's lap.

Trevor eyes the rather large bottle skeptically. "I feel like I should ask again if you plan on making my dick fall off during this trip."

Giggling, Skyler tells him, "I figured better safe than sorry. I really wouldn't want to ask the concierge to go get us more. Would you?"

"You're so thoughtful, baby," Trevor deadpans. But he takes the lube and carefully squeezes some onto his fingers.

Skyler very helpfully lifts up onto his knees to give Trevor better access to his ass, and Trevor wastes no time in finding Skyler's hole. He circles Skyler's rim with one fingertip, peppering Skyler's stomach with kisses while he does it. After only a few seconds, Skyler wants to sink right down on that finger. But Trevor's free hand is on his waist, urging him to stay up.

"I'd love to take my time playing with you," Trevor says, slowly slipping one finger inside, then sliding it back out and already adding another one. Skyler relishes the stretch. "I could keep you like this. Let you ride my hand, but not enough to make you come. I could wait until you're crying, begging me for your release before I fuck you. But we only have thirty minutes, so I guess we'd better make this hard and fast."

With that, he curls his fingers and nudges against Skyler's prostate. Skyler gasps, rocking his hips to feel more pressure there. He's riding Trevor's hand like Trevor said, and Trevor lets him. Trevor only stops him long enough to get a third finger stuffed inside Skyler's hole, and then Skyler goes back to working himself over.

"I'm ready, ready, ready," he chants. He slows enough for Trevor to remove his fingers, then he immediately reaches for Trevor's cock and lines it up with his stretched hole.

Trevor groans in pleasure as Skyler sinks down, taking it all at once. He said hard and fast, and Skyler has no problem with that. Although Trevor helps somewhat, guiding Skyler up and down by the hold on his hips and thrusting his own hips up occasionally, it's really Skyler doing all the work. And that's fine.

He loves working for it, hands on Trevor's shoulders, controlling the pace and angle, taking what he needs from his husband's cock.

It's not long before his thighs are burning from the effort, but he's so close. If he had more time, he could surely make himself come untouched, but they're on a time limit, so. "Touch me," he says. And Trevor doesn't waste any time in following the order.

All it takes is a few rough strokes and a twist of Trevor's wrist over Skyler's cockhead, and Skyler is shooting off between them. Skyler gazes down, his eyes just barely focused enough to watch as the white ropes land and slide down Trevor's abs.

And then Trevor takes over. Skyler slumps forward as Trevor starts thrusting his hips up forcefully while yanking Skyler's down at the same time. It leaves Skyler breathless, but he's happy to be used like this. Trevor grunts before his hips still and he holds Skyler tightly in place, his cock buried to the hilt in Skyler's ass as he releases into him.

"Check the time," Skyler says, finding the energy to grin down at Trevor. "I bet we could even go again before the food gets here."

He's definitely joking—he's worn out from that fuck and needs some time to recover—but it's fun playing the role of a sex fiend for Trevor. Well. He supposes it doesn't count as playing a role if he really *is* a sex fiend. It's not his fault he's addicted to getting off with his husband, okay? Trevor's hotness and skills are clearly to blame.

"Uh huh, sure," Trevor says. "How about we get dressed instead so we don't traumatize the concierge?"

Skyler shrugs that off. "I'm sure he's seen worse."

He gets up on shaky legs anyway, though, because he's nothing if not polite, and wanders off in search of the bathroom to get cleaned up. Trevor follows him, bringing all their discarded clothing. They probably don't have time to change into new outfits right now.

When the concierge escorted them into their bungalow, he offered to unpack and hang their clothes, but Skyler declined. Mostly because he couldn't wait to fuck Trevor, but also a little bit because he tries not to make people wait on him for things he could just as easily do himself.

After a quick wipe off, Skyler and Trevor make their way back into the main living area, and Skyler takes the chance to admire the aesthetics. Most of the furniture and décor seems to be made of bamboo and teakwood, with pristine white cushions anywhere a cushion is needed.

Well. The one on that chair might not be so pristine anymore.

The thought makes Skyler grin. When Trevor suggested they make time to take a vacation together, just the two of them, Skyler immediately showed his enthusiasm for that great idea with a blowjob. A preview of what was to come. So really, Trevor couldn't have been too surprised when Skyler jumped him as soon as they arrived, right?

They could've gone anywhere in the world, gone on some kind of crazy adventure if they wanted to. Lord knows, they can afford it. But they've already been around the world together. More than once. They've seen plenty of it.

Now they're only looking for relaxation, privacy, simplicity, and a little bit of luxury. And accommodations with a pretty view and plenty of surfaces to fuck on.

Okay, that last one might only have been Skyler's stipulation. But when Trevor found this Jamaican resort and Skyler saw the hammock in the photos of the bungalow's outdoor space, he was sold.

He'll need to check out the hammock later to see how sturdy it is.

SKYLER HAD AN INCREDIBLY RELAXING MORNING.. He and Trevor scheduled their couples massage for today, but Trevor surprised him by also scheduling Skyler for a facial and a manicure first. So he got his nails painted a light orange to go with the island vibes, they got their massages, and Skyler felt all pretty and pampered by the time they came back to the bungalow.

And now, after that sweet gesture, Trevor is torturing him.

They took the incredibly fluffy white duvet off the bed and laid it out on the floor in the main room, just because they could. Because they've already fucked in the bed, and this spot here seemed nice. If Skyler turns his head, he has a view of their outdoor area with the pool and built-in hot tub, and then the Caribbean Sea beyond that.

So yeah. It's a nice place to get fucked. Except Trevor isn't fucking him. Nope,

Trevor is being mean, taking him apart piece by piece with his fingers and tongue, but still not letting him come.

He's reduced Skyler to a whimpering, quivering mess.

Skyler's not above begging. In fact, Trevor often makes him beg, and Skyler loves it. But this time begging isn't getting him what he wants. He's tried and tried, and all of his pleas have been ignored.

"*Pleeeeease*," he tries again anyway. "I can't take it anymore."

"Are you sure, baby?" Trevor asks from his spot between Skyler's spread thighs. There's a hint of amusement in his tone at Skyler's pain. *Bastard.* "Am I not making you feel good?"

He's making him feel too good to the point of insanity, and Trevor knows that. He's currently got four fingers inside of Skyler, filling him up deliciously, but he's not going deep enough or fast enough to really satisfy him. And his other hand is playing with Skyler's balls, rolling and tugging on them gently, his thumb rubbing along the sensitive skin behind the sac. It feels good, but if he would just give Skyler *something*, something more to tip him over the edge . . .

Skyler shakily props himself up on his elbows to glare at his mean, mean husband. "If you don't let me come in the next two minutes, I'm going to do it myself."

He could have done that at any point, really. Grabbed his throbbing, leaking cock and given it a few swift jerks, and that would be it. Game over.

But maybe he actually loves Trevor's brand of torture.

When Trevor releases his balls to reach up and hold Skyler's hand, it settles the electrical current buzzing under Skyler's skin. He definitely loves his husband more than anything. Even if he's mean.

"I think you should just relax and enjoy this," Trevor says, "because there's no sex tomorrow."

"Wait, *what?*" Skyler cries, squeezing Trevor's hand harshly. "Why?"

"I want you to be able to ride the horses on Thursday," Trevor tells him, his fingers still moving torturously slowly in and out of Skyler's stretched hole. "And that won't feel good if you spend tomorrow riding my cock all day."

"Then I'll fuck *you*," Skyler declares. Problem solved.

Trevor chuckles. "I want to be able to ride the horses too."

Oh yeah. Logic.

"Damn," Skyler says in defeat.

Then he realizes that Trevor's distracted him from his current goal. Which is to come his fucking brains out right now, please and thank you very much.

He bends his knees and plants his feet on the floor to gain some leverage. When he starts fucking himself on Trevor's fingers, though, Trevor shakes his head and pulls them out.

"*Noooooo!*"

Skyler's going to go out of his mind. He really is. This is just cruel.

But then Trevor kisses the inside of his knee, running his clean hand up Skyler's thigh, and he shushes him in that special, soothing, Skyler-whisperer way he has. And everything in Skyler's head goes quiet.

"I've got you, baby," Trevor promises him.

When Trevor sucks the head of Skyler's cock into his mouth, Skyler doesn't try to urge him deeper. He just accepts what Trevor is giving him, because he knows his husband will take care of him like he always does.

Trevor carefully pushes his fingers back inside Skyler's hole, and although he still doesn't pick up the pace, he does go deeper and curls them, making sure they graze Skyler's prostate with every stroke. This, combined with Trevor's other hand moving steadily up and down Skyler's shaft as his tongue swirls around Skyler's cockhead, finally sends Skyler tumbling gently and blissfully over the edge.

Usually when Trevor makes him wait this long to come, it's explosive. But this is different. This time Skyler's orgasm washes over him in a haze of tranquility, leaving him feeling perfectly content, as well as aware of and connected with every molecule in his body. He feels weightless, like he wouldn't be surprised to find himself levitating a few inches off the floor.

He's aware of Trevor gently petting his side and telling him he'll be right back, but Skyler has no desire to move his head to watch where he's going. Trevor returns quickly with a warm, soft washcloth that he uses to wipe away the sticky lube from between Skyler's cheeks. And then Trevor lies down on his side, bracing himself up with one arm so he can smile down at Skyler.

He looks like an angel, and Skyler tries to smile back at him, but he's not entirely in control of his facial muscles yet.

"Love you," Skyler murmurs. So at least his voice is working.

"Love you too." Trevor leans down, cups the side of Skyler's face, and kisses him.

It's slow, sweet, and gentle. Exactly like the last hour has been. Possibly more? Skyler lost track of how long Trevor spent taking him apart.

They're so lucky to have the luxury of time now—which they never had when they were younger and in the band. And Skyler's grateful that Trevor loves him enough to want to spend that much time making him feel good.

He's grateful for a lot of things Trevor does for him. Like keeping him from spiraling with his anxious thoughts. Making him feel brave enough to conquer the world. Taking care of planning and all the little details so Skyler doesn't have to. Really, he's just grateful for Trevor being Trevor.

How damn lucky is he that he found the other half of his heart when he was only seventeen?

When Trevor rearranges them so that he's lying on his back, with Skyler's head resting on his chest and their arms around each other, Skyler isn't thinking about any of the other luxuries or activities this island has to offer. He could happily spend the rest of the day just like this.

The rest of his life, actually.

SWAYING GENTLY IN THE HAMMOCK, strumming an easy melody on his guitar, Skyler never wants this vacation to end. They could stay here forever, couldn't they? He wouldn't mind downsizing his house. Trading the view of the Pacific Ocean for the Caribbean Sea.

But he supposes he'd hate being even farther away from his family. He's been super looking forward to Thanksgiving next month, because his parents are coming to stay with him and Trevor for two weeks.

"Hey, did you book my parents their plane tickets yet?" he asks Trevor, who's lounging in a chair beside him, sipping a frozen margarita. Skyler's own pina colada is melting on the table, but he hasn't wanted to put his guitar down to drink it. This melody might be turning into something.

"No, I'll do it as soon as we get home. I just confirmed dates with your mom the other day."

Scrunching his forehead in confusion, Skyler asks, "The other day when?"

"When you were getting your manicure."

Now Skyler's amused. "You called my mom while we're on vacation?"

Trevor shrugs nonchalantly. "I wasn't going to miss it."

It's incredibly sweet how often Trevor talks to Skyler's mom. Even during the years Skyler and Trevor weren't together, Trevor still kept in contact with her. And since they got married, Trevor bumped up the phone calls to once a week. Honestly, Trevor talks to his mom more often than Skyler does.

"That sounds good," Trevor says. And at Skyler's questioning look, he gestures to the guitar Skyler's still absentmindedly playing.

"Oh, yeah." There are some lyrics floating around in Skyler's head, so he sings them as he continues to play.

Caribbean sunset
Frozen drinks by the pool
But the best part of paradise is being here with you
Horseback riding on the shore
Catered meals for two

That's where he's stuck.

He stops playing and frowns. "I don't have the next line."

Trevor appears to contemplate it for a few moments. Then he suggests, "When it's you and me, it doesn't matter what we do?"

"*Hmmm.* Maybe."

They play around with the lyrics for a bit, and Skyler loves this. He's been writing some songs here and there this year, whenever inspiration strikes. But nothing compares to writing love songs with the love of his life.

Except having sex with him, of course.

And it's their last night of vacation, so why aren't they having sex already?

"Uh oh," Trevor says.

"What?"

"You've got that dangerous look in your eyes again. You know, I'm starting to think you only love me for my dick."

Skyler laughs. "That's not true. I love you for your ass too."

Trevor gives him an unimpressed look, which only makes Skyler laugh again. Carefully extricating himself from the hammock, he sets his guitar on the table. Then he goes over to Trevor's lounger and manages to fit himself behind Trevor's back, his legs over either side of the chair.

He wraps his arms around his husband, resting his chin on his shoulder. "You're amazing, and I love you for exactly who you are. I love every single bit of you, not just the sexy parts."

"I don't know if I believe you," Trevor teases.

Skyler pinches his side. "Do I need to write a hundred more songs for you to prove it?"

Turning his head, Trevor gives him a warm smile. Their view of the sea has got nothing on the blue of Trevor's eyes. "You don't need to prove anything to me. You show me how much you love me every single day without even trying. Like it's something impossible to hide. And I hope I show how much I love you the same way."

"You do," Skyler tells him, leaning in for a kiss.

After a few seconds of kissing at an awkward angle, they rearrange themselves. Trevor turns all the way around, and Skyler stretches his legs out on the chair so Trevor can straddle him.

Like Skyler was trying to convey with the song lyrics, *this* is paradise. Being with this wonderful man—the sun to his stars, the honey for his bee—just getting to hold him, and kiss him, and love him . . .

Finally being able to do it freely is everything he ever wanted. No more of being urged into the closet and threatened into staying there. No fear of repercussions. Now they can love openly and proudly, because they fought for it.

And maybe winning their fight will make it easier for the next musician or actor or athlete to live their own truth without having to fight so hard. Every time the world sees queer people in love, maybe at least one more person will be able to recognize how beautiful that is.

That doesn't mean they don't still want their privacy. They don't need to make out in public for the whole world to see. But they can if they want to.

They *can.*

Having the privilege of making their love public makes loving Trevor in private feel even more meaningful. Their love means something to people. People they'll never even meet. And to Skyler, it means everything.

So Trevor can forgive him if it also makes him horny.

Skyler gets two handfuls of Trevor's ass and uses that as leverage to rock Trevor against him while he deepens their kiss, doing his best to devour Trevor's mouth. He wants to devour all of him.

It really does feel like the other half of his heart, or his soul, or whatever, is walking around separate from him. So he can't help it if he feels a constant need to connect his body with Trevor's. To have Trevor inside him or to be inside Trevor. Either way, that's how he feels completely whole.

He'd keep them connected like that all the time if he could, but he recognizes how this would make other aspects of living difficult. But they're on vacation. No work, no family, no friends, no bodyguards, no media. Obviously, he's going to take advantage of all this time to fuck his husband senseless.

"Remember when I said I love your ass too?" he asks, giving Trevor's cheeks a harder squeeze that makes Trevor jerk forward.

"Oh, you mean two minutes ago? Yeah." Trevor tangles both hands in Skyler's hair and tugs, giving Skyler the same rough treatment.

Skyler shivers when Trevor bites down on his neck, momentarily forgetting what he was about to say. Then he recovers, getting his own hand in Trevor's hair and yanking him back so that his husband can see the burning heat in his eyes. "I need to have it now."

Trevor laughs, even as his eyes blaze too. "I think that can be arranged. Where do you want me?"

It's hard to consider the possibilities when Trevor gets back to work sucking a mark into Skyler's neck. The easiest thing would be to do it right here, because they wouldn't have to get up, which means he could be inside Trevor more quickly. But they've already fooled around in these chairs plenty of times this week.

Skyler eyes the hammock. They did manage to have sex in it once. It was fun, but it was honestly a bit more complicated than worth it. And they had to do it nice and slowly, because they didn't want to risk falling out or breaking the thing.

Right now, he wants to take Trevor hard and fast. So he smacks him on the ass and says, "Get inside."

Trevor doesn't hesitate, which tells Skyler that his husband is just as horny for him as he is for Trevor. As if there were any doubts.

He practically chases Trevor into their bungalow, and Trevor laughs as Skyler crowds him up against the back of the couch. The laughter turns to a choked moan when Skyler places a firm hand between his shoulder blades and pushes down to bend Trevor over it.

"You might want to hold on to something," Skyler tells him, even though there's not much there to hold on to. The thin bamboo bar that runs along the top of the piece of furniture sits lower than the thick white cushions, and it doesn't seem entirely unbreakable, so he's glad when Trevor decides to curl his fingers into the material of the cushions instead.

Really, this is probably not the ideal location for a hard fuck. Skyler's vaguely worried about the entire couch sliding across the wood floor when he starts pounding into Trevor the way he intends to. But he hasn't had Trevor right here yet, and he was so keyed up coming inside that he didn't have the brain power to find a better spot. So whatever. If they scratch the floor, he'll pay to get it redone. He can take advantage of being rich sometimes, can't he?

"Baby," Trevor says, shoving his ass backward until it meets Skyler's groin. They're both in their swim shorts, so Skyler knows Trevor can feel how hard he is for him through the thin materials.

He thrusts forward once, just for fun, then says, "Don't move," and runs to grab the lube off the kitchen counter. That's where they left it after they had sex this morning.

When he returns to Trevor less than ten seconds later, he finds that Trevor's already removed his swim shorts and kicked them out of the way. The tantalizing sight of his husband bent over the couch with his bare ass sticking out—bare except for the small tattoo of the sun—makes Skyler go feral. He wastes no more time in shucking his own shorts and positioning himself with his hard cock nudging against that hot ass.

"How much prep do you need?"

The question is more of a courtesy than anything else. Because he knows his husband's body as well as he knows his own, and they have sex often enough that neither of them needs anything more than the most minimal prep. What he's really asking is how much Trevor *wants.*

"Just fuck me, baby," Trevor tells him. "You can't go all animal on me like this and then make me wait."

Skyler huffs, because they both know damn well that when the roles are reversed, Trevor will make him wait an eternity if he feels like it.

But he did ask, so he'll give his husband what he wants. He squirts some lube onto his fingers and moves them in fast circles around Trevor's hole. He dips one finger in, then promptly adds another, scissoring them to stretch Trevor's rim. And then he removes his hand, wipes it on the outside of his thigh, and uses both hands to grab Trevor's hips. His cock slips between Trevor's cheeks and finds Trevor's wet hole.

"You're *mine*," he growls as he pushes his way inside.

"Yours," Trevor grunts when Skyler's hips slap against his ass. "*Fuck.* That's it. Give me that cock, baby. Make me feel it for the whole flight home."

Well, okay. Challenge accepted.

Skyler establishes a hard and fast rhythm right away and never eases up. Just continues pounding into Trevor's tight hole, jerking Trevor's hips back roughly to meet every thrust. The couch does start to slide, but he can't be bothered to care. He steps forward with it and doesn't pause in his mission to fuck the breath out of his husband's lungs.

In only a short time, his orgasm starts to creep up on him, but he does his best to hold it back. He wants Trevor to get there first, and he really doesn't want this to end. But when he knows he can't hold off much longer, he lets go of one of Trevor's hips and reaches around to start tugging Trevor's cock at the same urgent pace that he's fucking into him.

"Oh, fuck," Trevor pants. "Yes. Yes. Don't stop."

Not if his life depended on it.

He keeps roughly jerking Trevor's cock, twisting, swiping his thumb across the head, until Trevor's entire body shudders and Skyler feels the warm, sticky release spurting out over his hand.

"Fuck, babe," Skyler says. "You're so fucking hot. Wanna stay inside you forever, but I'm gonna come."

"Do it. Give it to me," Trevor demands.

Those words break the tenuous control Skyler has over his body. His hips come to a stuttering stop, and he drapes himself over Trevor's back, biting down between Trevor's shoulder blades as he shoots his load inside of him. Trevor barely seems to register Skyler's teeth digging into his skin, because he's still breathing hard and recovering from his own orgasm.

With his clean hand, Skyler curls his fingers over Trevor's where they're still gripping the couch cushion. He gives himself a few moments before he straightens up and lets Trevor do the same. Neither of them seems ready to walk yet, though. Trevor's still got his back to him, so Skyler traces his finger along the edges of the tattoo behind Trevor's left shoulder. The one he got for his mom.

It's a gazebo, meant to look like the one in *Gilmore Girls.* Trevor's not a religious person, but he's told Skyler about how he pictures his mom there. Sitting in that gazebo, holding two cups of coffee, waiting for him. And someday he'll be able to meet her there.

As long as that day is very, very, very far away, Skyler wants that for him. So he imagines Stacey in the gazebo too.

He presses his lips there, then gently spins Trevor around to capture his mouth in a kiss much softer than the sex they just had.

After a shared shower, they carefully move the couch back into place, and now they're snuggled up on it when Skyler realizes something. "Before we leave," he says to Trevor, "can we have sex *on* the couch? We haven't done that yet."

How have they not done that yet?

Trevor laughs, turning to him with a smile. "Anything you want, baby."

Skyler kisses him. "*Best.*" Another kiss. "*Husband.*" One more. "*Ever.*" And he gives him another kiss for good measure, because really.

Best husband ever.

Best vacation ever.

NOVEMBER

SKYLER JAMES SHARES FAMILY THANKSGIVING PHOTO ON THE MEGA STAR'S SOCIAL MEDIA

TREVOR

IT'S CERTAINLY NO SECRET that Skyler loves to cook. So Trevor knew when he married him that Thanksgivings would be a big deal. Yet that doesn't stop his eyes from widening as he walks into the kitchen and sees every available surface covered with what looks like enough food to feed twenty-five people, rather than the seven they'll have. And this is after Skyler already cooked a huge breakfast for himself, Trevor, and his parents this morning.

Even when he checked on Skyler an hour ago to ask if he needed any help—and was promptly shooed away—Trevor didn't realize Skyler was making this much. He swears, if his husband wasn't born to be a pop star, he would've been born to be a chef.

"Baby, who do you think is going to eat all of this?" he asks with amusement.

Skyler spins around holding a ceramic baking dish between two oven-mitted hands. He's wearing his KISS THE COOK apron, so naturally Trevor has to walk over and give him a kiss. It's a rule.

Skyler carefully holds the dish out of the way to accept the kiss, and then he smiles sheepishly as he sets it down in the only available space left on the counter. "I know I may have gotten a little carried away, but there's no harm in cooking too much, right? Maybe we can bring whatever we don't eat to a homeless shelter?"

Trevor loves him for thinking of that.

"Yeah, of course." He spots a pot of carrots simmering on the stove, which he's sure Skyler's cooked with some kind of delicious honey glaze, so he reaches for the ladle, intending to snag some.

Skyler smacks his arm with the oven mitt he's just removed from his hand. "Don't you dare."

"I only want a couple. You've made plenty."

"Nope."

Cocking his head at him, Trevor asks sweetly, "For another kiss?"

While he halfway expects Skyler to tell him that Trevor damn well better kiss him for free whenever Skyler wants it, Skyler grins playfully. "Fine. One carrot for one kiss. And you need to pay up first."

With that demand, he puckers his lips, and Trevor happily fulfills his end of the deal. When Trevor pulls away, Skyler leans in for another quick kiss. Then he grabs the ladle before Trevor can, scooping up one lone carrot and holding it out for Trevor to take.

Trevor feels like he should argue that Skyler got two kisses, therefore he should get two carrots. But really, he'd give Skyler endless kisses for nothing.

After munching on the sweet vegetable, Trevor surveys the kitchen once more. Stella is lying on her dog bed in the corner, but she's alert, her nose twitching at all the food smells in the air. She's going to be thrilled when she realizes Skyler prepared a tiny, unseasoned portion of all the foods that are safe for dogs to eat, because he wanted her to have a Thanksgiving dinner too.

"Are you sure you don't need any help in here?" Trevor asks his ridiculously thoughtful husband.

"I appreciate it, but I'm good," Skyler assures him. "Everything is just about ready to go. Are Noah and Jasper here yet?"

"They're both on their way. They should be here any minute."

"Good," Skyler says. "I hope everyone's hungry now. I'm keeping a bunch of stuff warm in the chafing dishes, but as soon as this turkey comes out of the oven, I want to be ready to serve."

"You at least need to let me help you bring the food into the dining room when it's time," Trevor tells him. He and Theresa set the table with dishes and silverware earlier, but that's the only help they've been allowed to give so far. They've spent the rest of the morning watching the parade on TV with Skyler's dad.

Agreeing to that offer, Skyler sends Trevor away so he can finish getting everything ready. Trevor figures he should get back to the living room before Jasper arrives anyway, because he doesn't want him to feel awkward.

He invited Jasper just last week, when he learned Jasper doesn't have family in the area and didn't have any plans for the holiday. In the time they've been working together, Trevor has begun to suspect that Jasper doesn't really have anyone supporting him, which sucks. So he really wants Jasper to understand that Trevor can be more to him than the guy who signed him a fairly large check to make an album.

Trevor spent those awful years after he and Skyler broke up without much of a support system, and now that he's lucky enough to have such a wonderful group of family and friends in his life, he'll gladly spread the warmth to other people who need it.

Plus, Skyler would've killed him if he found out Trevor let Jasper spend Thanksgiving alone. Skyler would probably try to feed the entirety of L.A. County if they showed up at his gate today.

Jasper arrives first. He promptly removes his leather jacket, and underneath, he's wearing a long-sleeved black button-up that he looks quite uncomfortable in. Trevor's guessing he wore it in some misguided attempt at being polite.

This poor guy. First, he tried to dress down for them, and now he's trying to dress up. Trevor wishes he understood that he can just be himself.

Nobody is formal here. Skyler's planning to change into a nicer outfit before dinner, but that's only because Skyler will jump at any chance to plan an outfit. And Trevor's just wearing jeans and a T-shirt.

Trevor introduces Jasper to Skyler's parents, and Theresa immediately starts engaging Jasper in conversation. It's obvious, at least to Trevor, how much she's trying to make him feel comfortable and welcome. Clearly, Skyler takes after her in this way. Although Ben is equally as kind; he's just a slightly more reserved person, so making endless small talk isn't his forte.

Noah shows up five minutes later, also in jeans and a T-shirt. Since his parents are still traveling, it was obvious he'd come here for dinner. He greets Skyler's parents warmly, then frowns when he spots Jasper. Trevor wishes he'd get over whatever his issue is with him. The guy has been nothing but nice and respectful to Noah, and Noah still hasn't dropped his thinly veiled layer of hostility.

At least he quickly turns his frown into a forced smile, giving Jasper a simple nod and a muttered, "Hi."

"Hey," Jasper replies, sounding more sincere. "Good to see you again outside of the studio."

Whether or not Jasper truly means that, Trevor isn't sure, but he's absolutely certain that Noah's clipped response of, "Yeah, you too," is an utter lie.

Thankfully, before any more strained pleasantries are attempted, Skyler flounces into the room wearing fitted tan slacks and a short-sleeved white button-up that's covered in tiny turkeys. Trevor has to hold back a laugh, because that isn't what he expected when Skyler said he was going to wear something nice. But honestly, it probably should've been. Where did Skyler even find a shirt like that?

He's got the first few buttons undone, and he's not wearing an undershirt, showing off peeks of some of his tattoos. Trevor wonders if it's weird to find a man wearing turkeys so attractive.

"Dinner's ready!" Skyler announces exuberantly. "Come on!"

Everyone gets up and follows as he leads them into the dining room. As their guests take seats, Trevor and Skyler head back to the kitchen to start bringing out the food. It takes more than a few trips, but Skyler won't let anyone else help.

Once their feast is spread out on the massive dining room table, Skyler's dad carves the turkey, then everyone starts loading up their plates. Trevor hopes the tension between Noah and Jasper will be less awkward now that people are busy stuffing their faces. Or at least less obvious.

Jasper notices the other empty plate at the table and asks if anyone else is joining them.

"It's for Hal," Skyler explains. "Mike took the day off, because his sister is hosting dinner at her house. So he's over there. Hal didn't mind staying here, and I invited him to eat with us, but he said he'd be happy to just grab some food and take it back to his apartment to watch the game. I already texted him to come get it whenever he wants."

"Well, you've certainly made enough, sweetie," Theresa says. "This all looks delicious."

Beaming with pride, Skyler thanks her. Then he jumps up from his seat. "Oh! We should all share something we're thankful for!"

This proclamation is met with some groans and eye rolls, but Skyler just grins at everyone, completely undeterred in his mission to fulfill holiday traditions.

"I'll go first," he says, and he only has to pause a second to think of his answer. "I'm grateful to have a career that lets me share my passion with the world, and to have so many awesome fans who have continued to support me after I came out."

Trevor smiles, because it's impossible not to smile at Skyler when he's being so sweetly sincere. But then Skyler catches his eye and grins cheekily before adding, "And I'm grateful that my husband is so hot."

Okay, so much for the sweet sincerity.

"How touching," Ben deadpans as Skyler sits back down, still looking pleased with himself. Then, when there are a few beats of silence in which it seems like nobody else is going to comply with Skyler's request, his dad sighs and stands. "I'm grateful that my two wonderful, intelligent, caring children are both successful, happy, and healthy."

Skyler smiles at that, but Trevor knows he'd be happier if Layla could've flown in for the holiday too. Unfortunately, she couldn't get the time off from the hospital, since the Thanksgiving and Christmas holidays tend to bring in more emergencies than normal.

After Ben retakes his seat, Skyler's mom stands up with a dinner roll in her hand. "I'm grateful for having a son who's a better cook than me, so that I didn't have to spend all day in the kitchen preparing this meal."

Everyone laughs, and she winks at Skyler before sitting down.

Jasper glances between Trevor and Noah, as if waiting to see if either of them will go next. But Trevor is still trying to figure out what he wants to say. There are so many things he's grateful for, and he knows he could simply pick any one of them, but he wants to take Skyler's request seriously.

Clearing his throat and looking awkward, Jasper stands. "Uh. First, I want to say thank you to Trevor and Skyler for inviting me here. And I'm grateful to Trevor for taking a chance and signing me, and I'm even more grateful to be working with a label that actually cares about their artists beyond how much money they can make off them."

Noah grunts, and Trevor kicks him under the table. Jasper quickly sits back down as Noah stands. Looking first at Skyler, then at Trevor, Noah says, "I'm grateful for second chances and the friendships I've rebuilt. And for how well the record label is doing."

Trevor gives him a nod of acknowledgement. Sometimes he thinks the label means more to Noah than it does to him. And it means a hell of a lot to him. Of course, it's also possible that Noah might be using all his work for the label as a means of avoiding the rest of his life. All year long, Trevor's felt like something is off with him.

But he can't dwell on that right now, because he realizes he's the only one left to say something. And he still hasn't quite found the right words to express everything he's grateful for. He's grateful to be married to Skyler, obviously. But he's also grateful for all the other love and support that being with Skyler brought into his life. He's grateful to Theresa for being there for him like a mother would ever since he lost his own mother. He's grateful to have Ben and Layla too. And even Mike and Hal, who have become friends.

And the other guys from the band, of course. He's so grateful for the strong bond the five of them have, but he almost lost that. If he and Skyler hadn't gotten back together, Trevor doubts he would've gotten Noah and Jermaine back in his life either. Who knows how long he would have kept himself isolated?

Standing, he locks eyes with Skyler and doesn't look away. "I am so beyond grateful that Skyler James decided to sit down next to me that day at auditions all those years ago. Because I don't want to imagine what my life would look like now if he hadn't, but it certainly wouldn't be filled with this much love."

Skyler's eyes look a bit teary as he reaches across the table over all the food for Trevor's hand. He squeezes it, and Trevor squeezes back before he sits down.

Hopefully, that encompassed everything.

EVEN THOUGH SKYLER WAS DETERMINED not to let his parents help clean up, his mom pulled rank and told him to go hang out with his dad while she took care of the kitchen. Noah and Jasper didn't stay too long after dessert, so as soon as they were gone, Skyler and Ben started a game of Scrabble, and Trevor jumped in to help Theresa.

He didn't mind taking care of the dishes after Skyler did all that work cooking. And luckily, Skyler had already gotten a few pans soaking and started one load in the dishwasher before they ate.

Spending time alone with Theresa is something Trevor relishes anyway, so this is nice. They talk on the phone all the time, but seeing her in person is better. Receiving her warm smiles and getting to hug her whenever he wants.

She's been like a mom to him all these years, especially after he lost his own mom. But he's never thought of her as a replacement. She's her own person, and he appreciates her for who she is. And nobody could replace his mom.

"What's wrong, hon?"

Trevor glances up to find Theresa watching him, her brow crinkled in concern, and realizes he zoned out. His intention was to scrub down the pan in the sink, but he's not sure how long he's just been standing here clutching the sponge in his fist.

"Just thinking about my mom," he confesses.

"Aw, hon." Theresa comes closer and pulls him in sideways, kissing his temple.

Trevor offers her a sad smile. "But I was also thinking about how lucky I am to have you in my life."

"Trevor."

The gentle way she says his name makes him drop the sponge into the sink. After drying his hands on a dish towel, he turns to her fully.

Sighing softly, she says, "When Sky had us sharing what we're grateful for, I made a joke out of mine. But I could have said something else. I could have said how grateful I am that my son has a wonderful husband who loves him and does anything to make him happy. I could have said how I'm grateful that the man I've always considered a son has now officially become my son."

There's suddenly a lump lodged in Trevor's throat. He clears it, but he still can't find the words to say how that makes him feel. When Theresa reaches out, her fingers grazing the back of his hand, he has to swallow again and will himself not to get teary. Finally, he manages a lame, "Thank you."

"You don't need to thank me. It's the truth."

He engulfs her petite body in a hug, humming in contentment when she wraps her arms around his waist. They stay like that probably a few seconds longer than necessary, then she rubs her hand up and down his back before letting go.

As they step apart, Trevor feels like he should say something else. He's supposed to be good with words. If he could sit down and try to write this into a song, he might have a better shot at conveying his emotions. But he's pretty sure any attempt at saying more to her right now will only get him choked up again.

Thankfully, Theresa spares him by silently returning to the cleaning.

As they're finishing up, she suggests they make some tea. So Trevor fills the electric kettle and grabs the fancy little wooden box Skyler uses to hold the tea bags. After the water heats, they each fix their own teas. Then they end up leaning over opposite sides of the island, cradling warm mugs and chatting about little things. Like the new book club Theresa started at the library, and a true crime docuseries they both watched.

"So I promise I'm not rushing you," Theresa says slowly, after a brief lull in the conversation, "but have you and Sky discussed any more plans for having kids? You guys told me you talked about it, and that you both decided it's something you want. But have you thought it through any further?"

Trevor runs his thumb along the rim of his mug, recalling the not-quite-an-argument he and Skyler had and how they temporarily resolved it. The topic has come up a couple other times since then. Skyler promised he's okay with waiting at least a few more years. But Trevor's sure he'd be overjoyed to start filling this house with children right now if they could figure out a way to make it work with their current schedules. Unfortunately, they haven't been able to. Not yet.

"I don't think we'll be in the position to start seriously considering it any time soon."

"Why not?" Theresa asks, frowning slightly.

"We're both just too busy," Trevor tells her. "And neither of us is willing to give up our careers yet, or even slow them down."

Skyler has had a fairly low-key year, but Trevor knows he'll be itching to tour again soon. That man can't stay away from the stage for too long.

"That's understandable," Theresa says as she neatly arranges the two cartoon turkey figurines Skyler put out as holiday decorations. "Though it's not like you can't afford childcare."

"It's not about the money. More that it doesn't seem right to bring children into our lives only to let some random nanny raise them."

She doesn't respond to that right away. So for a few moments, they both sip their tea in silence. But her face suggests she's working through something, and then—"What if it wasn't a stranger?"

Trevor cocks his head to the side. "What do you mean?"

"Well . . ." Theresa brings her tea with her as she comes around to his side of the counter. Then she sets the mug down and leans her hip against the edge. He turns sideways to face her, bracing himself with one forearm on the countertop. "I haven't mentioned this to Sky yet, but Ben and I have been considering some changes in our lives. Thanks to all the help Skyler's given us, we think we can afford to retire early. Or at least I can."

"Wow, that's great." Trevor's happy for her. He and Skyler wouldn't hesitate to pay all of Theresa and Ben's expenses, but they'd never accept that. At least Skyler paying off their house and buying them each new cars years ago has helped them get ahead.

Theresa smiles and sets her hand on his arm, giving it a squeeze. "I really enjoy being a librarian, so it's not as if I'm desperate to quit my job. But what I would love more than anything is to be closer to my three children."

It takes Trevor a second to understand that she's including him when she says *three* children, and this time there's no stopping him from getting choked up. Not even a glance at the silly turkeys helps. "We'd love to see you more often," he says, voice wavering as he tries to hold back the tears from spilling. "That would be great."

"Now obviously, with you two and Layla on opposite sides of the country, we know we can't be close to all of you at the same time." Theresa pauses, giving his arm one more squeeze before letting it go. "But if I retired and Ben and I moved out here, he could likely find a teaching position at a college nearby. Then we'd be able to go stay in New York with Layla during the summer and winter breaks if we wanted to."

Trevor nods. "Absolutely. And you know you're always welcome to stay in our apartment there to give Layla more space."

"Thank you, hon," Theresa says. She takes a sip of her tea, then smiles at him. "But the point I'm trying to make is . . . if you and Sky decided you wanted to grow your family sooner rather than later . . ."

As she trails off, Trevor puts together the pieces of what she's saying. "You want to help us?"

"I would *love* to help you," she tells him. "You don't even need to consider it me helping you. I'd be delighted to have some grandchildren to take care of."

"Wow." Trevor's pretty sure he already said that a minute ago, but this calls for a repeat of the sentiment. Because yeah. What she's offering really might be the key to him and Skyler getting to have everything they want all at once.

Theresa cups his chin in her hand and leans in to give him a motherly kiss on the forehead. "It's just something for you two to think about. Nothing has to happen right away. But like I said, Ben and I have already been considering a move. So we could probably make this happen fairly quickly if you needed us to."

"Thank you." He doesn't know what else to say. "Seriously. We would never ask you to give up your house and your lives in Ohio for us, but if it's something you want, then this sounds amazing. *Thank you.*"

"You don't have to thank me, hon. That's what family is for."

DECEMBER

SUN & STAR RECORDS ORGANIZES SURPRISE CHRISTMAS CONCERTS AT LOCAL HOMELESS SHELTERS

SKYLER

SKYLER BEGAN DECORATING FOR CHRISTMAS on the first of December. He started out small, just placing figurines on some shelves, figuring Trevor wouldn't notice. Not that Trevor would mind. Now, by the middle of the month, this house is so festive, it could probably give Santa's workshop at the North Pole a run for its money.

While Skyler loves living in Malibu, one thing he really misses about growing up in Ohio is actually having snow for Christmas. He could do without it for the rest of winter, but the holiday doesn't quite feel the same when it's sixty degrees and sunny.

He can't do anything about the weather, but he can sure as hell fill his own house with Christmas spirit. Right now, he's got holiday music playing over the sound system, and he's singing along while he throws a few extra decorations on the tree.

"Hello, my little Christmas elf."

Standing on the ladder, Skyler twists around and smiles at the sight of Trevor, who just got home from work and is still wearing his sexy business attire. "Hi!"

"Please be careful up there, baby," Trevor tells him.

Skyler rolls his eyes. "I'm like four feet off the floor."

"True. But I'm afraid if you add any more decorations to that tree, it might topple over and crush you."

The tree doesn't have *that* much on it. But Skyler gets his point. He should probably stop adding things before it goes from sparkling and beautiful to blinding and garish.

He turns back to the tree to hang the glittery snowman ornament he's holding, then carefully steps down the ladder. Trevor holds out a hand to steady him, and once Skyler's feet are planted firmly on the floor, Trevor spins him by his waist and meets him for a kiss.

"It smells really strongly like cinnamon in here again," Trevor comments as they head upstairs so he can change. "Did you buy more of those pinecones?"

"I made Snickerdoodles!" Skyler says innocently. Which is true, but if this explanation for the delicious cinnamon scent lets him avoid admitting that he *did* buy more pinecones, then he's going to take advantage of it. "They should still be warm for you."

Trevor smiles softly at him as he unbuttons his shirt in their bedroom, but there's a keen spark in his eye that suggests Skyler's not fooling him. Oh well.

Stepping closer, Skyler nudges Trevor's fingers away so he can be the one to undo the last couple buttons and slide the shirt off Trevor's muscular shoulders. "I just want the house to really feel like Christmas."

"It definitely already does, baby," Trevor tells him, giving him another kiss. "But you can keep decorating as much as you want. Whatever makes you happy."

Skyler gets started on Trevor's belt next. What would make him the happiest is if he and Trevor had a few kids they could surprise on Christmas morning and shower with presents. That's obviously not their reality for this year. Maybe one year soon, though.

After learning that his parents want to move to L.A. and will be able to help him and Trevor once they do have children, Skyler's hopes have grown higher and higher. He understands there's still no need to rush things, but having that potential plan makes it feel like they're one step closer to being dads.

The sound of Trevor's leather belt sliding out of his belt loops as Skyler tugs on it gets Skyler feeling a little frisky. So once he's tossed the belt to the floor, he quickly gets Trevor's pants undone, then reaches in to palm Trevor's soft cock over his black boxer-briefs. It doesn't take more than a few seconds of rubbing before Trevor starts to harden, his cock now straining against the tight fabric.

"Let's get that free," Skyler suggests, nudging Trevor's pants down over his hips and then carefully peeling the briefs over his erection.

Trevor steps out of both, leaving him standing gloriously naked for Skyler at the foot of their bed. "Aren't you such a good Santa's little helper?" he teases.

Skyler grins and lowers to his knees. Grabbing Trevor's hips, he presses a kiss to one, then leaves a trail of them along Trevor's vee as he makes his way toward his reward. His tongue darts out to lick at Trevor's cockhead, making Trevor suck in a sharp breath. And when Skyler wraps his lips around it, both of Trevor's hands come to the back of Skyler's head. There's not enough pressure to hold him there, but it's enough to encourage Skyler to take him a little deeper.

As he sucks his husband off, he slides his palms from Trevor's hips down to his thighs, giving them a light squeeze. The slightly salty taste of precum hits his tongue when he runs it again over Trevor's slit. Humming in enjoyment, Skyler begins licking circles around the head of Trevor's cock like he's trying to catch ice cream dripping from a cone.

He could take Trevor's entire thick cock down his throat and get him off in just a couple minutes if he wanted to. But instead, he's keeping this blowjob slow and sweet, savoring it.

Trevor tangles his fingers into Skyler's hair and tugs gently. "Come up here, baby. I wanna touch you."

Pulling his mouth off Trevor's cock, Skyler looks up at him from his knees. No matter how long they're together, he'll never get tired of the sight of his hot, naked husband standing over him like this. Trevor leaves one hand in Skyler's hair and uses the other to cradle his face. For another moment, they stay just like that, smiling at each other like they're sharing a silent secret.

When Trevor tugs Skyler's hair again, Skyler takes the hint and stands. Burying both hands back in Skyler's hair, Trevor pulls him in for a long, languid kiss. They lick their way into each other's mouths and work on getting Skyler out of his clothes without disconnecting their lips.

They do a decent job until they inevitably need to pause the kissing so Skyler's shirt can come over his head. Then Trevor spits into his own palm and lines up their cocks, wrapping his hand around both. He immediately starts stroking them at a rough, rapid pace.

So much for slow and sweet. Not that Skyler's complaining.

Nope. No complaints here. Never any complaints whenever Trevor is touching him.

They resume kissing, but more aggressively now, biting and tugging on each other's lips to match the vigorous way Trevor is working over their cocks. Skyler's knees start to tremble, so he pushes at Trevor's chest, urging him onto the bed. Trevor complies, relinquishing his grip on their cocks as they situate themselves with

Trevor on his back and Skyler on top of him. Once they're settled, Trevor spits into his hand again and gets it wrapped back around both of them.

Skyler groans in pleasure, his hips rocking forward without his permission, thrusting his cock farther into Trevor's grip. His orgasm is nearing already, and he wants Trevor to get there with him. "I'm close," he says.

"Me too," Trevor tells him. "Give me that mouth, baby."

Skyler doesn't need to be told twice. But Trevor brings his free hand to the back of Skyler's neck anyway, pulling him down into the kiss as if Skyler wasn't moving fast enough for him.

The feel of their slick cocks gliding together as Trevor jerks them has Skyler panting into Trevor's mouth. And then Trevor lets go of Skyler's neck and reaches down to grab his ass cheek instead, using his grip to encourage the motion of Skyler's hips. Skyler can only take a few moments of this before he's ripping his mouth from Trevor's and coming with a shout.

Trevor's hips thrust up, and he squeezes Skyler's ass hard as he follows him over the edge. "*Fuuuck*, baby."

Collapsing his body on top of Trevor, Skyler can feel both of their releases making an even bigger mess between them. But he can't be bothered to care as Trevor rubs his back with his clean hand while they catch their breath.

After a few minutes, Trevor smacks him on the ass and says, "I want your cookies now. Can you put on a sexy little elf costume and bring me some?"

He's joking, but little does he know that Skyler *does* have a sexy elf costume. He was saving it to wear on Christmas Eve, but why not get as much holiday fun out of it as he can?"

"Wait here," he instructs, giving Trevor a quick kiss before hopping off the bed. Trevor sends him a puzzled look, but Skyler ignores it. He dashes into the bathroom, where he uses a wet washcloth to clean himself up, then he brings another out for Trevor, tossing it to him before running into their closet.

Two minutes later, he emerges with a wide grin, feeling pretty pleased with himself. He's wearing a green and silver striped tank top that's cropped above his belly button, a velvet green skirt with a fuzzy white trim along the bottom, and a pair of green tights. And to top off his fantastic outfit, he's got on a headband that gives him elf ears.

Trevor's eyes go wide at the sight of him, then they darken with lust.

"I'm not bringing the cookies up to you," Skyler tells him sassily. "So you'd better put some pants on and come downstairs with me."

At first, Trevor doesn't move. But when Skyler turns for the door and shakes his ass a couple times, his husband springs into action.

Skyler gives him the courtesy of waiting while Trevor tugs on a pair of gray sweatpants. Then he yells, "Catch me if you can!" and sprints out of the bedroom, giggling at the sound of Trevor right on his heels.

They slow down on the stairs, because Skyler is definitely clumsy enough to fall, but as soon as he starts running again, Trevor resumes chasing him. Stella is barking from somewhere in the house, probably wanting to know what the hell all the noise is for. When Skyler makes it into the kitchen, he pauses, allowing Trevor to capture him in his arms.

Sneaking one hand up the back of Skyler's skirt, Trevor palms his ass over the tights. "You are ridiculous, and hot, and I love you." He gives Skyler's ass a hard squeeze. "Now where's my cookies, little elf?"

Skyler gently shoves him off so he can go over to the baking sheet he left on top of the stove. The Christmas music is still playing down here, so he dances along to it as he transfers the cookies onto a large plate.

"If you keep shaking your ass like that, I'm gonna have to eat it instead of the cookies," Trevor warns him.

Grinning to himself, Skyler eases up on the dancing. Because as tempting as that sounds—and it sounds *very* tempting—he still needs to get started with making dinner.

Stella's nails clack on the floor as she enters the kitchen. When Skyler turns to her, her ears shoot backward. She looks terrified, so he takes off his elf ears and sets them on the counter. No longer concerned, she trots over to him, her nose twitching at the smell of food.

"Don't worry, girl," he tells her. "I made doggy cookies too."

Taking a seat at the island, Trevor asks, "You made treats for her?"

Skyler grins at him. "Yeah! They're shaped like candy canes!"

Trevor shakes his head, but his smile is adoring. "You are the cutest husband ever."

"I also bought her some reindeer antlers. But I guess I won't torture her with making her wear them until Christmas morning. I want to get a picture of the three of us in front of the tree."

"I'm sure she'll keep them on long enough to take a picture at least before she starts trying to knock them off," Trevor says, eyeing the dog.

Skyler grabs two of the large homemade treats from the counter and feeds one to Stella, leaving the other on the floor at her feet. Then he finishes plating up the snickerdoodles and brings the plate over to the island, setting it in front of Trevor.

Reaching for him, Trevor pulls him down so that Skyler's half-perched on his lap. He snags a cookie and offers Skyler a bite before he tries it himself. They sit there a few minutes, feeding each other. It would be terribly cute and innocent—if it weren't for Trevor's free hand casually migrating underneath Skyler's skirt and rubbing his thigh.

Damn, Skyler's happy.

Like he's so incredibly happy right now that he doesn't know what to do with himself. He almost wants to go run a lap outside or jump in the pool to let out some of the giddiness inside of him. But he stays exactly where he is. Quietly singing along to the Christmas music and letting his husband feel him up while feeding him cookies. What a perfect evening.

A little while later, as Trevor's helping Skyler with dinner, he tells him, "I'm going to start putting some presents under the tree. Promise you won't pick them up and try to figure out what they are."

Skyler fake-gasps. "I would never!"

"Oh, please," Trevor says. "I know you."

With a shrug, Skyler pokes at the broccoli he's sauteing. That's probably fair. He has been known to do that before. It's not that he wants to ruin the surprise, but he gets so excited, he acts like a little kid sometimes. Really, though, he likes giving presents even more than he likes receiving them. And he tends to go overboard.

Trevor kisses the back of Skyler's head as he crosses behind him to the fridge. The gesture makes Skyler smile, but just as quickly, his smile fades. Because now he's thinking about all the kids in foster homes, and kids staying with their families in homeless shelters. There are so many kids out there who might not be getting any presents for Christmas, either because they don't have parents or their parents can't afford to buy them. And here Skyler is, blowing as much money as he wants on unnecessary decorations, and flouncing around in a silly elf costume like everything's merry and bright.

While for some people, the holidays only remind them of everything they *don't* have.

"Baby?" Trevor says with a tinge of concern in his voice.

Skyler turns to him. "Huh?"

"You're staring at that broccoli like it's the worst thing you've ever seen."

"Oh." Shaking his head, Skyler turns off the burner. The broccoli looks done enough. "I just . . . I wish we had kids to spoil for Christmas."

"Aw, baby." Trevor winds an arm around Skyler's waist. "We will someday. I promise."

Skyler nods. "I know. But actually, what I was really thinking about is how unfair it is that there's so many kids out there without families right now who won't get a Christmas. And all the families living in shelters. Can you imagine spending Christmas surrounded by strangers and no one's getting presents?"

Trevor frowns and is quiet for a minute as Skyler finishes with their dinner. Then suddenly, he says, "Well, what if we did something for them this year?"

"What? Who?" Skyler asks.

"We can't help everyone in the world. But we could do something at the local shelters. Bring food and presents."

Skyler jumps at that idea. "We totally should! That would be awesome!"

"Yeah," Trevor says, setting two plates on the counter. "I could use the record label to put something together. Not just make donations, but maybe I can organize surprise little concerts at different shelters on Christmas Day."

"Oh my god, yes! I'll sing! And I bet Oli would love to." Skyler's mind is racing excitedly now. "And you have to sing too, of course. And Noah."

"And I'll ask Jasper to do it," Trevor adds. "And a couple of my other artists. I'll talk to Courtney about it. I wouldn't necessarily want a lot of publicity for this. It should be about doing something nice for the families. But she'll probably think it's a great idea to put the label's name behind it."

Skyler kisses him. He has to. His husband is incredible.

He knows they can't help everyone. The world is full of people in need. But he and Trevor are fortunate enough that they have an abundance of money and resources to spare. If they can bring a little bit of joy to people's lives, they definitely should. He can't wait.

And just like that, Skyler's Christmas spirit is back.

TREVOR

TREVOR IS FUCKING EXHAUSTED. Slumping down low on the couch, he fears his body is going to melt all the way into it. Actually, no. He might just be okay with that.

He's been on world tours with Boys Will Be Boys. Performed in a different city every night, while also doing interviews and recording new music whenever they weren't on stage. And yet, after this one Christmas Day, he's possibly more wiped out than he's ever been before.

A lot went into planning and coordinating people for the surprise shelter appearances. Especially because he was putting it together at the last minute. And then actually doing it, bringing the food and toys, meeting all the people and singing for them . . . it was a lot all in one day.

They didn't all go to every shelter. Trevor split everyone up into small groups of two or three and mapped it out so that they could cover as much of L.A. County as possible. They managed to hit more than twenty-five shelters between everybody, and Trevor made additional monetary donations to each of them.

It felt great. Using his wealth for a good cause, bringing some measure of joy to people who are going through awful times. And seeing the joy on Skyler's face made Trevor happy too. Trevor tried not to rush him away at each stop, but Skyler could've spent all day talking to each child he met. He even taught one teenage boy how to play a couple chords on his guitar, and it was unclear who was more excited about this.

Trevor's going to love being a parent with that man someday.

"Eggnog for you and hot chocolate for me," Skyler announces as he comes into the room with a glass in one hand and a mug in the other. Stella's padding along behind him, probably hoping he has food. He passes Trevor the eggnog before plopping down on the other end of the couch and stretching his legs out over Trevor's lap.

Trevor starts massaging his feet with his free hand, and Skyler hums his appreciation. "Thanks, baby," Trevor tells him. "But you might have to carry me up to bed after this. I'm so beat that one drink might be enough to knock me out."

"I can do that," Skyler says.

Trevor laughs. "I'm kidding."

"Hey!" Skyler kicks one foot gently into Trevor's stomach. "I could totally carry you!"

Maybe he could. Skyler works hard to keep himself in shape for performing the way he does, and he's much stronger than he looks at first. If people saw him naked, they'd notice all his muscle definition, but of course, only Trevor gets that pleasure.

Still, though. Carrying Trevor, who is definitely bigger than him, all the way through the house and up the stairs would be crazy.

"Yes, you're very strong," Trevor says, making it obvious he's placating him.

Skyler glares, but then he wiggles his feet and smiles when Trevor goes back to rubbing them.

Trevor sucks down half of his eggnog and leans forward over Skyler's legs to set the glass on the table, freeing up both hands to use on Skyler. He kneads the soles of his feet, eliciting a pleased moan, and then he moves upward, squeezing Skyler's calves.

There's a colorful beaded bracelet on Skyler's wrist that Trevor's pretty sure he's never seen before. It looks like children's jewelry. "What's that?" he asks, pointing to it.

Skyler grins and gives the bracelet a twist around his wrist. "A little girl at one of the shelters gave it to me! She was too sweet. I mean, she's living in this shelter, so I'm sure she doesn't have much, but she still wanted to share with me."

"Kids are good like that."

"I felt bad taking it," Skyler goes on. "But I also didn't want to reject her offer of friendship, so I traded her one of my rings."

Oh geez. Trevor gives him a disbelieving look, and Skyler shrugs.

"It wasn't a very expensive one."

Shaking his head, Trevor tells him, "*You're* too sweet."

Skyler shrugs again. "It's only jewelry. I'd never give away any of the ones you gave me."

"I know you wouldn't, baby."

"I'm just really glad we got to do something nice for all those kids."

"Me too," Trevor agrees.

Skyler shakes his entire legs this time, and Trevor obligingly resumes the massage. When Skyler finishes his hot chocolate, he sets the mug down and moves to cuddle up against Trevor's chest. Trevor wraps his arm around him, trailing fingers up and down under the sleeve of Skyler's shirt. He'd be content with staying exactly like this forever if they could.

"*Mmm*," Skyler murmurs softly, as if reading Trevor's mind. "Feels good to be home."

Trevor kisses the top of his head, knowing Skyler's not only talking about being in their house after a long day. He means being under Trevor's arm. He's referencing the tattoo of a house that Trevor got in that spot for him all those years ago. When Trevor promised to be his home.

And Trevor's so proud of the way he was finally able to keep that promise.

"I changed my mind," Skyler says after a minute, squeezing Trevor around the middle and snuggling in even closer. "I want *you* to carry *me* up to bed."

"Lazy baby," Trevor teases affectionately. "I thought you were so strong."

"I am. I'm strong like a superhero. I could still totally carry you. But I figured this way would be good practice for you for when we have kids. So I'm doing you a favor, really."

The lame attempt at justification makes Trevor chuckle. And he imagines he'll actually have to fight Skyler for the privilege of carrying their future sleeping children up to bed when the time comes.

He ruffles Skyler's hair. "All right, we really should get up now. I think we need to shower before bed after all we've done today."

"Hmm, I vote no on that," Skyler says.

"Come on, baby," Trevor urges, poking him in the side until Skyler jolts away.

"Okay, okay. But I still expect to be carried."

Trevor points to the cups on the coffee table. "How about you bring those to the sink, and I'll go up and turn on the water?"

Skyler eyes him distastefully, then stands with a dramatic sigh. "*Ughhh*, fine. Less than two years of marriage and he stops giving me whatever I want. Sheesh, what a rip off."

As Skyler bends down to grab the cups, Trevor smacks his ass. Hard. "Brat."

Laughing now, Skyler turns around and gives him a kiss. "Go on. I'll meet you upstairs."

When Trevor heads for the stairs, Stella gets up from her giant dog bed to follow him. The spoiled girl basically has her own bedroom upstairs, but she'll still go into theirs at night as long as they're not having sex too loudly.

This will definitely be a quiet night. Trevor's dead on his feet as he gets undressed and lets the shower warm up, but he still wants to wash off the day before he gets into bed.

Skyler joins him in the bathroom a minute later. He lets Trevor strip him and guide him into their large walk-in shower. Once they're standing under the rainfall showerhead, Trevor releases a long, tired sigh. Skyler grabs his own body wash, but Trevor takes it from him and gets to work, lathering the sweet-smelling stuff onto his husband's skin. He doesn't care how tired he is. He always wants to take care of his baby.

After they're both clean, they step out of the shower and dry each other off, exchanging slow, syrupy kisses as they do it. Then they finally make their way into bed. Stella's already asleep on her bed in the corner, but Trevor won't be surprised if he finds her in bed with them when he wakes up.

As Skyler gets settled lying on his side, he scoots his ass backward until he's pushing up against Trevor's body. Taking the hint, Trevor rolls over to spoon him. And Trevor's last thought before he falls asleep is that he must be the luckiest man in the world. Because he gets to end his long days like this, with the love of his life wrapped in his arms.

JANUARY

SKYLER JAMES WALKS RED CARPET WITH HUSBAND TREVOR BLUE FOR THE PREMIERE OF *THE PRINCE'S JOURNEY*

TREVOR

"WHAT IF ONE OF THOSE AWFUL right-wing groups shows up to protest?" Skyler asks nervously, breaking the last five minutes of silence in the back of the limo.

When he woke up this morning, he was excited for the premiere. He's been talking animatedly about it all day. But Trevor noticed Skyler's mood was more subdued while they were getting ready, and since they started the drive to the theater, his tension has become increasingly obvious, though he insisted he was fine when Trevor asked.

Placing a hand on Skyler's bouncing knee, Trevor assures him, "There's going to be plenty of security. Nobody will get close enough to protest."

There's been some noise online, of course. Assholes making a fuss about Hollywood corrupting children. The usual bullshit. And Trevor has encouraged Skyler to do his best to avoid looking at any of that. Overall, though, the response to the film's announcement has seemed positive. Once people actually watch the film, Trevor's hoping even more will be won over by it.

Not that he's seen it himself yet, but from the parts of the script he's read with Skyler, he's sure it's going to be great. And how could anyone not be charmed by a cartoon version of Skyler?

Skyler is still frowning and twisting one of his rings around his finger, so Trevor takes his hand and gives it a supportive squeeze. He gets a small, grateful smile in return. Then Skyler says, "I just want people to like it."

"They *will.* Your fans are going to love it. So many children are going to love it. And you know there's no point in trying to please the homophobes, right? All we can do is ignore them, let them be miserable, and continue being who we are."

As Trevor reminds Skyler of this important truth, he's aware that Skyler learned how to do it way before Trevor did. Skyler's style and choices have always garnered more criticism than Trevor's, and that didn't stop him from coming out. It may have taken Trevor longer, but he got there too, and he's never going back to being afraid.

"It's not only that," Skyler says quietly. "I know it's an animated film, and I'm only voice acting. But it's still *acting*, which is something I haven't done since I was a teenager."

Oh. Trevor feels like an ass for not picking up on this sooner. He knows Skyler's worried about the perception of the movie because it's a queer children's movie, and doing a good job was so important to him because he wanted to present a character that queer children could feel represented by. But naturally, Skyler wants his acting ability to stand on its own, too.

"Baby, I spent hours reading lines with you," Trevor reminds him. "And you are a fantastic actor. I'm sure you did an amazing job. I can't wait to watch the film tonight and get to see everything come to life."

Skyler nods, but his body still shows signs of tension. Trevor hasn't really seen him like this since way back at the beginning of the band days, when he would freak out right before a performance or an interview.

But Trevor hasn't forgotten what to do. He slips his hand from Skyler's so that he can move it up and wrap it firmly around the nape of Skyler's neck.

The effect is immediate. Skyler takes a deep breath, and then his body relaxes. Everything about him softens. Especially his gorgeous green eyes when he looks at Trevor. "I love you so fucking much."

"I love you too, baby. And if you get on that red carpet and start feeling like you don't belong there, you can just think about the fact that you have a star tattooed on your ass cheek."

Skyler's joyful laughter bursts out of him, and Trevor's glad he could bring some levity here. But he wants Skyler to know how serious he is too.

"You've always been my star," he says, rubbing his thumb up and down along the back of Skyler's neck. "And you always will be."

"Thank you." Skyler leans over and kisses him, his tongue slipping briefly inside Trevor's mouth before he pulls away.

Trevor takes his hand again. "Really though, I want you to remember one thing. No matter what happens tonight, I'll be by your side the entire time. And after the event is over, you'll still be my husband, and I'll still love you. And then we'll get to go home to where it's only you and me, and nobody else's opinions can touch us there."

Skyler gazes at him for a few moments, his eyes brimming with love. Then he asks, "How do you always know the perfect thing to say?"

"I think that's just the magic of being with your soulmate."

A goofy grin takes over Skyler's face. "Because you and me, we're a beautiful symphony. Lovestruck serenades, your heart sings to me."

Trevor gives a fake groan. "And then you have to listen to your soulmate being cheesy and quoting his own song lyrics to you."

"Yup," Skyler says happily. "And it's all I wanna hear for the rest of my life, the sounds of our sweet soulmate symphony."

"Me too, baby," Trevor tells him truthfully. "Me too."

The rest of the limo ride is filled with kisses and private laughter. They'll be facing the world tonight, and they'll get to be themselves, get to show off their love. But this right here—who they are in the little moments—is what really matters.

TREVOR STEPS OUT OF THE LIMO FIRST to the shouts and the camera flashes. The media circus is waiting for Skyler, but photographers are clearly not opposed to getting shots of him too. Turning back to the limo, Trevor extends his hand to help Skyler out of it. The shouts grow louder and more enthused as Skyler emerges, looking absolutely stunning in a long-sleeved, dark purple, suede jumpsuit. He smiles broadly, effortlessly spinning around as his name is called out from different directions. There's no trace of the nerves he showed Trevor on the ride.

Hand-in-hand, they walk the red carpet, until someone in charge asks Skyler to step forward so the cameras can get a few shots of him alone. But Trevor stays close waiting for him, and when they're instructed to keep moving, Skyler reaches his hand back and Trevor takes it, stepping up to his side again.

Up front by the theater, Trevor is allowed to stay beside Skyler for more photos, and even for a few quick interviews. Skyler continues to grin like he doesn't have a care in the world as he graciously answers the media's questions. And the whole time, Trevor is there by his side. Like he promised.

Just like he should've been right from the beginning, if so many people hadn't worked so hard to prevent that. At least now, finally, he can support his husband publicly and proudly. They don't have to hide their love like it's something shameful.

This is the way things were always meant to be.

After they're dismissed to make room for the next celebrity, Trevor and Skyler head to the lounge for the pre-show cocktails, hors d'oeuvres, and mingling. Trevor chats with a few people, but mostly, he just stands back watching with awe and pride at the way Skyler can captivate anyone, simply by being himself.

It's not like he didn't already know Skyler could do that. Even as a teenager, Skyler's presence captivated Trevor immediately, didn't it? But it's still an incredible thing to witness. Especially in a setting like this, where he knows Skyler feels at least a little bit out of his comfort zone. Where the majority of the guests are from the film industry, not the music industry.

Considering this is an animated film, Trevor didn't expect the event to be so star-studded. He knows there's a couple of big-name actors in the cast, but he's surprised at all the other well-known actors not associated with the film who are here tonight.

Skyler introduces Trevor to his costar, Ryan Brinkley, who's been working as a Broadway performer for the past few years. This is his first film role. Trevor has only heard one song from *The Prince's Journey* so far—a duet between Skyler and Ryan that the director sent to Skyler—but that was enough for him to gauge how talented of a singer Ryan is.

When he tells the man as much, Ryan blushes and casts his eyes downward. "Thank you. But we all know who the star of this movie is. I swear I almost pissed myself when I heard I got cast alongside Skyler James." He lifts his head and manages to send a weak smile Skyler's way. "Eighteen-year-old me definitely would have."

Trevor can't tell if Ryan's admiration for Skyler is strictly on a professional level, or if there's a bit of a crush lurking behind it too. He wouldn't be mad if there was—he couldn't blame the guy—but he'd also like to prevent the conversation from veering in that direction before it gets awkward.

Skyler just laughs though. "And eighteen-year-old me probably would've pissed myself if I found out I'd be working with a Broadway star. I was a major theater kid before I ended up in Boys Will Be Boys."

"I'm certainly not a star," Ryan replies, shrugging one shoulder as if to downplay his talent. "The highest I've made it is fourth on the cast sheet."

"I bet you'll be landing some lead roles after this," Skyler tells him. Then, gesturing around the room, he asks, "Unless you want to keep working in film instead of Broadway?"

Ryan shrugs again. "I think I'll probably go back to Broadway, but my agent is going to try to get me more auditions for film roles too. I'd be down for anything as long as I get to sing."

And here, Trevor steps in. "Have you ever considered singing on its own as an option?"

"What do you mean?" Ryan asks him with a slight downturn of his mouth.

Trevor pulls out his wallet, rifles through to find a business card, then hands it to him. "I'm not sure if you know that I own a record label. I can't promise you anything. I've only heard one of your songs, but like I said, your voice is great. If you're interested in the idea of potentially making an album, we should talk more."

Ryan's eyes go wide. "Wow, damn. Um. I mean, yeah. Maybe. I've never really thought about it, honestly. I'm afraid I'm not a songwriter."

"Not a requirement," Trevor assures him. While his preference is for working with artists who write at least some of their own music, he could easily work with ones who don't. He's already been hiring some very talented songwriters to help his artists, and he still enjoys writing himself.

And he hasn't had the chance to help shape an artist in that way yet. To work with someone in finding the right genre of music, the right types of songs to highlight their voice, and to pair them with songwriters who will give them lyrics they connect with. It might be cool to try it.

"Well, I'll definitely keep this in mind," Ryan says, smiling shyly as he tucks the card into his back pocket. "Thank you again."

After Ryan wanders off a minute later, Skyler turns to grin at Trevor, nudging him in the side with his elbow. "Look at you networking. That was hot. My super sexy, bigshot businessman label owner."

Trevor snorts. "Is that what I am?"

"Mmhmm." Skyler grabs his hand and raises it between them to kiss the back of it. "You were already super sexy before you started the label, of course. But watching you pass out your business card makes me wanna drag you off and find the bathroom."

"And what would you plan on doing with me in there?" Trevor asks playfully.

"Oh, I can think of so many things."

Trevor brings their hands up to his own mouth to give Skyler's a kiss. "As fun as that sounds, I'd rather you not get kicked out of your first Hollywood premiere before the screening even starts."

Skyler pretends to consider this. "I dunno. Might be worth it."

"Behave," Trevor warns him.

That makes Skyler groan quietly and duck his head into Trevor's shoulder. "Don't use that voice on me. It's *not* going to help discourage me."

Laughing, Trevor pats him on the back. "Come on. Let's find some more people for you to charm the pants off of."

"Still not helping," Skyler mumbles, but he follows Trevor's lead as they head over toward a small group of celebrities neither of them has met yet.

Pretty soon, someone makes an announcement directing everyone to head into the theater and take their seats. An usher leads Skyler and Trevor to theirs, and as they get settled, it appears Skyler's nerves have returned. He starts fidgeting with his ring again, his knee bouncing in the dimly lit theater.

Trevor knows Skyler wouldn't want anyone else to see him like this, so he quickly places his hand around the back of Skyler's neck.

"*Magic*," Skyler sighs out as he stills. And when Trevor removes his hand a few moments later, Skyler reaches for it, drawing it into his lap where he can trace over the tiny, tattooed *S* that sits in the space between Trevor's thumb and index finger.

Trevor lets him keep playing with his hand as the director stands up in front of the screen and says a few words, thanking everyone for their hard work on the film. Then the man sits down in the front row, and a few moments later, the movie starts.

Seeing Skyler as an animated character is surreal. Even though Skyler only provided the voice, it's clear that the artists modeled the character's look after Skyler. Trevor joked a while ago, when Skyler first got the role, that he might end up attracted to a cartoon version of him. And, well . . . he won't say he's actually attracted to the cartoon, but the character *is* gorgeous. Just like the man who inspired it.

The movie is just as good as he expected it to be. Not that children's movies are his favorite, but the message is important. The representation matters. The prince's character is unabashedly queer from the start, and the king and queen accept him fully, which is so refreshing to see.

Trevor's not ashamed to admit he almost tears up at the emotional plotline. At the way the prince pursues the peasant boy, but the boy needs to learn how to embrace his own sexuality the way the prince has before he's ready to face the kingdom as the prince's love.

As he watches the movie, Trevor can't help sneaking constant glances at Skyler, whose face is lit up with a combination of joy and awe the entire time. And that makes Trevor so happy. His baby deserves this.

By the time the movie ends, though, and they've made their way over to the afterparty, Trevor is sort of ready to be done socializing and just get home where he can relax. But this is Skyler's night, so he forces himself to perk up. He fulfills his role of the doting husband without complaint—because that's truly what he is—but still, he's relieved when Skyler decides he's had enough and is ready to go.

They're both a little tipsy at this point, and if this were ten years ago, they might have started fooling around in the back of the limo on the way home. Now, they're too mature for that. Although that doesn't stop Skyler from placing his hand obscenely high on Trevor's thigh and teasing him with it for the entire ride.

But it's okay. When they get home, Trevor will make him pay for that in a way they'll both enjoy.

FEBRUARY

SKYLER JAMES FANS WONDER WHEN THEY'LL GET THE SINGER'S NEXT ALBUM

SKYLER

"YOU KNOW," TREVOR PANTS OUT as he pounds into Skyler's ass, "we won't be able to fuck all over the house like this once we have kids."

"We can if they're babies," Skyler counters, breathing heavily himself. "At least while they're sleeping."

Trevor shakes his head. "Not sure it's gonna work like that."

"Do we really wanna talk about this right *nooow?*" Skyler asks, the last word turning into a moan as Trevor nails his prostate just right.

They're in their home gym, where Trevor found him finishing up his morning workout. Skyler's currently flat on his back on a weight bench, with his legs up by his ears, because Trevor's pressing down on the backs of his thighs for leverage. Not that he needs more leverage. Both of Trevor's feet are planted on the floor, and he's basically using Skyler's ass as a seat.

"No," Trevor relents, both on the topic and on his hard, aggressive fucking into Skyler's hole. He slows his pace enough to give Skyler a chance to catch his breath. "Just thinking about it."

"Well, stop thinking," Skyler demands, purposefully squeezing his muscles around Trevor's cock. "And finish fucking me."

Trevor gives him a dark look that makes every part of Skyler tingle, and then he thrusts his hips so hard it probably would have knocked Skyler off the bench if Trevor didn't have such a good grip on his legs.

"*Unf, yes, more,*" Skyler whines. "Come on. Do it like you mean it."

He's purposely goading his husband now, and Trevor responds with a hard smack to the inside of Skyler's thigh.

"Oh god, yeah, please. Give it to me."

This earns him a matching smack to the other thigh. The heat radiates far past the area of skin Trevor has hit. It burns all through Skyler's body, lighting him on fire.

Trevor keeps up with the punishing thrusts, adding a few more smacks that are sure to leave Skyler's skin flushed red. And he loves it. He'll be thinking of this crazy hot sex while he's sitting in his boring meeting this afternoon. Feeling the twinge in his ass as he listens to people asking him for the hundredth time when he's going to finish his next album.

"Fuck, baby," Trevor says. "You feel so good around my cock. I can't last any longer."

"Go on, fill me up," Skyler encourages him. "I want it. Make my hole all messy, and then you can lick it clean."

With a groan that sounds almost pained, Trevor's hips smack against Skyler's ass one more time, and then he stills, flooding Skyler's hole with his warm release.

"Jesus." Trevor slumps against Skyler's body. "I think it's your filthy mouth that needs to be cleaned out."

Skyler just grins at him. Then he whines and rocks his hips as much as he can from this position, hoping to remind his husband that he still hasn't come yet. Before he can voice a complaint, Trevor is sliding his softening cock out of Skyler's hole and replacing it with his tongue. Skyler gasps, letting his shaky legs finally come down to rest over Trevor's shoulders. Good thing he stretched before his workout, because Trevor sure kept him bent in half for a while.

He reaches for his neglected cock and starts jerking himself while Trevor licks and sucks at his hole, sliding his tongue in and out of it. From the noises he's making, Skyler can only assume that Trevor is, in fact, doing his best to eat his own cum out of Skyler's ass.

Fuck.

That's so hot.

Trevor obviously doesn't mind that Skyler is sweaty from his workout and the rough fucking he just took. Because he's moaning like Skyler's the best thing he's ever tasted. His grip on Skyler's ass cheeks is hard enough he might be leaving red marks there to match the ones on Skyler's thighs.

Skyler's tugging his cock at a slow but steady pace. He's been right on the edge since Trevor first slammed into him, and he knows if he goes too fast now, it'll be all over within seconds. He wants a minute to enjoy this.

But when Trevor takes his mouth off Skyler's hole and rasps out, "Come for me, baby," Skyler's body listens. With one more rough tug of his cock, he lets out a moan and shoots onto his stomach.

He continues touching himself softly as he comes down from his orgasm, vaguely aware of Trevor's tongue swiping a few more times over his hole. He's still in a bit of a sex daze as Trevor stands and holds out a hand to help him up.

"How come you're not at the office?" he asks.

"I didn't have any meetings or anything today," Trevor explains. "So I texted Noah to let him know I was taking the morning off. I made you some breakfast, but then I came to find you and got, uh, kind of distracted."

At Trevor's sheepish shrug, Skyler laughs. "I think I'll take an orgasm and cold eggs over no orgasm and hot eggs. Any day."

"Next time, I'll plan better so you can have both," Trevor tells him.

Skyler beams at him. "You're such a good husband."

He needs to hurry if he's going to eat something, grab a shower, and still make it on time to his meeting, though. So he hustles Trevor out of the gym and toward the kitchen. While Trevor pops some eggs and turkey bacon into the microwave, Skyler takes a seat on one of the stools, immediately wincing, because *yeah*, he's a little sore.

And he has absolutely no regrets.

AFTER THE MEETING WITH HIS LABEL AND MANAGEMENT, Skyler's refusing to do anything productive for the rest of the day. He's not sure why this particular meeting put him in such a weird mood. It went exactly as he expected it to, with questions about when he plans to finish the album, if he has any more songs for them to hear, if he wants them to get some other writers working on it.

Does he intend to take more time off to do other movies?

What direction does he see his career heading in?

And it's that last question that's really got him overthinking things. Because when you're in the crazy lucky position where you can have pretty much anything you want, you actually need to figure out what you want.

Skyler has always been the kind of person who wants too many things. He can't help it if he falls in love with everything he does. He's passionate and greedy like that.

It's not like he's stopped making music. He's been in the studio multiple times. He has enough songs recorded to make up half of a new album, but so far, nothing cohesive is really coming together. And maybe that's because it feels like he's been in some sort of limbo this year. Like he's on the verge of transitioning into a new phase of his life, but he's not quite there yet.

Whatever is stalling him, though, it doesn't matter. His label is getting antsy. They were cool with him taking the time to do the voice acting role, because they know drawing attention to him in a new medium will boost his music sales too. But what if he wants to keep acting? What if he wants to try more than voice acting? If he landed a role in a live action film, then that would involve a much longer time commitment that would keep him away from doing music.

He's always loved both. Singing and acting. Singing is his number one passion, but he loved getting the chance to exercise other talents this year. And this could be his chance to gain some momentum in the film industry.

The idea of having kids with Trevor has also been on his mind a lot lately. He understands why it crossed Trevor's mind even while they were having sex. Because they've been doing their research and getting themselves prepared for it. They've debated the idea of using a surrogate to have a baby, versus adopting a slightly older child through the state, and they've looked into both. They found the most highly recommended surrogacy clinic in the area, and they learned the steps they'd need to take to get licensed for adoption.

But they still haven't made any decisions about *when* they want to take this huge step.

It feels like they could start the process any time they choose to. Financially, of course, they're all set. And with Skyler's parents deciding for sure that they're moving out here, they know they'd have plenty of help.

Last month, Skyler's parents told him and Trevor that they had officially put their house on the market and were looking for a place near them. And Trevor ended up offering them his mom's house in Santa Monica, which seems perfect for everyone. Trevor couldn't bring himself to sell it when he moved in with Skyler, and now he's so happy that it won't be sitting there empty anymore.

So Skyler and Trevor could get this family ball rolling whenever they want to.

But are they really ready to change their lives in such a major way? There's no rush, as Trevor keeps reminding him.

And it's true. It's just that Skyler feels so torn. He's absolutely certain he wants to have kids with Trevor, and he feels more than ready to be a father. What he's not entirely ready to do is give up having Trevor all to himself. Not quite yet.

This whole situation is part of what's holding him back from finishing his next album. After he releases a new album, he'll need to go on tour for it. And this time, Trevor won't be able to come with him. At least not for the whole thing, like he did with the last one. Because Trevor's got the label to run, and things are really picking up for him with that. Skyler can be selfish sometimes, but he wouldn't try to take Trevor away from his own passion.

God, his head is such a jumble of thoughts right now. This is why he'll never give up on writing songs, even if he's wondering about where his career will go next. Songwriting is an intrinsic part of who he is. It's how he lets his feelings free so that they don't take up all the space in his head. He needs that expressive outlet.

But there's also this weird feeling of repetition that's been bothering him lately. He's been doing the music thing for so long now. First with the band, and then solo. Going solo was a big change, and although he loved singing with the band, the change was really good for him. But now he's been doing it solo for long enough, too, that he's starting to feel stuck in a cycle of rinse and repeat again. Like back then when the band was being forced to keep churning out albums.

And this is how he's spent his day while he's been waiting for Trevor to get back home. Stuck in his own head, thinking himself in circles and getting nowhere.

So when Trevor comes in the door, Skyler doesn't wait to pounce on him. Because the best way to turn his brain off and make it all go blissfully quiet is to lose himself in the man he loves.

"Well, hey to you too," Trevor says with a smile, after Skyler kisses him in the entryway. "I take it you missed me?"

"Always," Skyler answers truthfully. As if Trevor doesn't already know.

Taking Skyler's face in his hands, Trevor kisses the tip of his nose. "I always miss you too, baby."

Skyler leans in and starts kissing Trevor's neck as he works on unbuttoning his shirt. Trevor lets out a pleased sigh, tilting his head to give him better access. But then he brings his hands up to cover Skyler's, which impedes Skyler's progress on getting him undressed.

"How was your meeting today?" Trevor asks, laughing softly at Skyler's whining and attempts to bat his hands away.

Shaking his head, Skyler tells him, "Same. Boring. Too many questions. Please get naked now."

"Since when am I not allowed to ask you questions?"

Skyler sighs and turns to walk out of the entryway, letting Trevor come farther into the house. "I didn't mean you. I'm sorry. At the meeting they asked too many questions that I don't have answers to."

"Well, I would ask you to tell me more," Trevor says, taking his hand, "but I'm guessing you'd rather do something else right now, and talk to me about it later?"

At Skyler's nod, Trevor gives him a quick kiss, then leads him upstairs.

Just having his hand linked with Trevor's has already settled some of the anxiety inside Skyler. Because Trevor has always made him feel safe. Trevor offers him love and acceptance, security and support. And he asks for so little in return.

But Skyler does his best every day to give Trevor those things too. He wants to give Trevor everything.

He knows that every healthy relationship is a give and take, but it doesn't even feel like that with them. It feels like magic. The way they fit together so effortlessly. Complete each other. They way that all they have to do is be together, and it feels like they're each giving what the other one needs.

Right now, what Skyler needs is to make love to his husband. He needs to remember that no matter what, he's not alone.

And even though Trevor will encourage him to make his decisions about his career based on what's best for him alone, Skyler knows that what's best for him is really whatever is best for *them.* Because they're together in the forever sense, and Skyler will never have to be alone again. That makes everything feel easier.

Talking with Trevor will help him figure things out.

After orgasms.

In their bedroom, they strip each other slowly, kissing as they do it. The urgency Skyler felt when he first met Trevor at the door has faded, and now everything between them is syrupy goodness.

Trevor gently twirls Skyler's hair around his fingers.

Skyler brings Trevor's forearm to his mouth, licking over the tattoo there, as if he can taste the sweet honey dripping from the wand.

Trevor ducks his head down and swirls his tongue around each of Skyler's nipples, coaxing the buds to harden.

Skyler's fingertips dance along Trevor's hipbones.

By the time they're lying in bed together, Skyler's mind is nothing but a haze of bliss, and they've barely even done anything sexual.

Then Trevor reaches for Skyler's erection, and Skyler gasps, instinctually thrusting his hips to start sliding his cock in and out of the circle of Trevor's grip. Trevor runs his thumb over the tip, smiling when Skyler's cock kicks in response. "Do you want me to top, or do you want to top me?"

Skyler whines and shakes his head. "I don't know. God, please don't make me choose." He's been so bad at decisions today.

"Okay, baby, no problem," Trevor says. "Don't worry. I won't make you choose."

And Skyler's relieved that Trevor understands. Although he wouldn't expect anything less, because Trevor always knows what Skyler needs. Even when Skyler doesn't.

Apparently, what Skyler needs tonight is to be worshipped. To be kissed all over his body until every inch of skin is tingling. And then he needs Trevor to slide two thick fingers inside him, to stretch him just a little bit in preparation. Since he's already been fucked earlier today, and it doesn't take much to get him ready for Trevor's cock.

When Trevor fills him up with it, he leaves no room for anything else. No thoughts, no doubts, no future plans. Just this. Just his husband. Just what he needs.

Skyler's lost to the sensations Trevor is causing in him. Lost to the slow, steady thrusts, the kisses, and the occasional easy strokes of Skyler's cock. They're moving together, breathing in sync, eyes open, pouring all their love into each other. And when they come, they do it together, riding the waves of pleasure for what feels like an eternity.

And it is.

Because when you're this connected to another person and you love this strongly, it lasts forever.

MARCH

WHAT'S NEXT FOR MUSIC'S POWER COUPLE SKYLER JAMES AND TREVOR BLUE?

TREVOR

TREVOR RUBS AT HIS EYES, giving them a brief break from staring at the computer screen as he reads through proposed contract changes. This is probably his least favorite part of owning his own label. Sorting through legalese, negotiating, consid-ering money. Looking out for his own best interests while also trying to hold the artists' best interests in mind. Basically, the business part of the business.

That's not to say he's not good at it, and luckily, his small legal team already understands the ways he likes to operate, so that makes things easier. But he prefers to spend his time focusing on helping people make music.

Right after he has finished initialing one contract and he's about to open anoth-er, there's a single knock that makes him look up. Noah is standing in his office doorway with a strange, concerning look on his face.

"What's up?" Trevor asks warily. The last thing he wants to deal with before he gets to go home today is some kind of crisis. Like a computer error that lost an artist's entire album recording file. That happened last week, and thank god, an IT guy was able to recover it, but it left Trevor with a stress headache for two days.

Noah shifts his weight, leaning against the doorframe. "Uh, I was just wondering if you and Sky had plans for dinner."

That wasn't what Trevor was expecting. He frowns in thought and glances down at his phone. Skyler hasn't texted asking him to pick up any takeout on his way home, which most likely means he's planning to cook something.

"Not really, I don't think. I mean, nothing special, at least. Skyler's probably cooking."

"I figured I should have asked earlier," Noah says, reaching up to adjust his tie. "But I was busy and . . . Anyway, would you mind checking with him? If he's already started, then I don't want to bother you guys. But I was hoping you might want to come by my place for dinner? I'll cook."

Trevor furrows his brow. "Why? You hate cooking."

A look crosses Noah's face like he might turn around and flee, but then he says, "True, yeah. It's just that I wanted to talk to you about something. Something kind of important."

And now Trevor almost wishes he was only here to report a computer emergency. Because what other kind of thing could be important enough that Noah needs to talk to him about it over dinner? They talk every day here in the offices. A great deal of their conversations are about work, but they're still friends. They talk about their personal stuff too.

Or Trevor does, at least. Noah hasn't really had anything too personal to share in a long time. Which has only increased Trevor's worries that Noah's overworking himself and not allowing himself to have a life outside of this business. He's been afraid Noah will burn himself out, and maybe that's what this is about. Maybe he's gotten tired of putting so much of his time and effort into Trevor's dream.

"If you can't do it tonight, don't worry about it," Noah says when Trevor fails to give him a response. "Like I said, I should've asked you earlier. We can do it another night."

Trevor shakes his head. "No, no, it's fine. Um. Lemme just call Sky. But how about you come to our place instead? I'm sure he's already preparing something, but he won't mind cooking for one more."

"Are you sure?" Noah asks. The hopeful tone in his voice is hard to miss.

"Yeah, no worries. I'll call him, and I'll let you know what time he wants you to come."

Noah nods. "Thanks. I'll at least bring over a bottle of wine. Ask him if he has any preferences."

"Okay, will do," Trevor tells him. Then with one more nod, Noah turns and walks off, presumably to his own office. Trevor gets up and shuts his door before he dials Skyler.

Skyler answers the phone and immediately starts recounting for him a conversation he just had with Layla about a guy she's dating. As if he's the one who called Trevor.

Trevor listens to the story of how the guy had been trying to hide his roommate from Layla for a totally unclear reason, but then Layla learned the truth in a way that involved nudity. The roommate's, not hers.

Once Skyler's done laughing about it, Trevor tells him, "Hey, so Noah asked if he could come over for dinner tonight."

"He invited himself for dinner?"

"Well, actually,"—Trevor leans back in his chair, crossing one leg on top of the other—"he invited us over to his place for dinner. But I know he can't cook to save his life, so I wisely volunteered your culinary skills. I did it for you, really, so you wouldn't be subjected to a plate of burnt meatloaf or something."

Skyler laughs. "Aw, thanks, dear. You're so sweet."

"I know."

"Is there a reason he wants to have dinner with us, though?"

Yeah, apparently there is. And that's what's worrying Trevor.

"He said he wanted to talk to us about something important. No idea what." Trevor grabs a pen off his desk for something to fidget with. "Honestly, I'm a little worried he wants to quit the label. He's been acting strange all year. I know I've told you how much he's thrown himself into the job."

"True," Skyler says. "But it seems like he *wants* to spend his time working. It's not like you asked him to help you out to make the label happen. He came to you about it."

"Yeah, and I'm so glad he did," Trevor admits. "I planned to do this whole thing by myself, but having him with me on it has been a lifesaver. I would've lost my mind trying to handle all this work on my own. And now that I officially made him VP, I can't imagine losing him. But I'm telling you, he's seemed extra off lately. Unhappy, even."

"Okay, why don't we wait and see what he wants to talk to us about before you start worrying too much. It's probably something else entirely. Because if it's just about work, then why would he want to talk to me too?"

Oh, yeah. That's a good point. But Trevor can't imagine what else it could be. He knows Noah's parents are still off traveling the world, and it seems like Noah barely talks to them anymore. Maybe he misses them and wants to go meet up with them for a while?

Skyler's right, though. There's no use in speculating about what's going on when they'll find out in a few hours.

"You don't mind cooking dinner for three?" he double-checks.

"Not at all."

With the plans set, Trevor hangs up and tries to get back to focusing on contracts. But they're even harder to get through now.

THERE'S MUSIC PLAYING WHEN TREVOR GETS HOME. That's probably how he makes it all the way into the kitchen undetected, where he catches Skyler bopping along to the beat as he stands at the stove.

"Smells good in here, baby," Trevor says, wrapping his arms around Skyler's middle.

Skyler jumps at the contact, but Trevor's hold on him keeps him in place. He cranes his neck back for a kiss, which Trevor gladly leans in to give him. "Thanks. It's just a shrimp stir fry. I figured we didn't need anything fancy, since we wanna focus on whatever it is that Noah needs to tell us."

Skyler's hair is up in a very messy bun, so Trevor twirls one of the hanging pieces around his finger before massaging Skyler's nape. Skyler moans softly and leans into the touch.

Trevor presses a kiss to the back of Skyler's neck that makes his husband shiver. "I appreciate you doing this on short notice."

"It's totally not a big deal," Skyler assures him. "I would've already had a dinner started when you called, but I lost track of time working on a song."

"Oh yeah?" Trevor asks, always interested to hear when Skyler's writing new stuff. "For your next album?"

Shrugging, Skyler says, "I guess. I dunno, really. For some reason, that's still not quite coming together. Like thematically."

"Do you think it has something to do with the way you've been feeling this year? With so many things being open-ended for you?"

The look Skyler gives him when he turns around in Trevor's arms tells Trevor how much he appreciates being understood. "I think that's exactly the problem. And believe me, I'm grateful I have so many different opportunities and choices I could make for my life right now. But yeah. It's made me a little all over the place with the songs I'm coming up with."

"You'll figure out what you want to do, baby. You always do."

"Because I've got you on my side."

"Damn straight you do. Forever."

Skyler grins. "Forever sounds really good."

They share a long kiss, Trevor trying to lick the taste of coconut off Skyler's lips until Skyler giggles and pushes him away. Then Trevor runs upstairs to change into more casual clothes, and by the time he gets back downstairs, Noah has texted that he's on his way.

When Trevor opens the door for him, Noah holds up an expensive-looking bottle of wine, the smile he tries for not quite reaching his eyes. Trevor accepts the wine and tells him, "Come on in. Sky said dinner will be ready in a minute."

"Great." Noah sounds like he's being led to his death, rather than the dinner table.

They make their way through the house and into the kitchen, where Noah says hi to Skyler and Trevor grabs three glasses to pour the wine. Skyler lets them know he's about to plate up the meal, and he tells them to go chill in the dining room to wait. He insists he can carry all three plates himself, so Trevor and Noah do as instructed. But Trevor cowardly wishes Skyler needed help, just so he wouldn't have to sit alone in this awkwardness with Noah.

This is dumb. Noah is one of his closest friends. Why are they being like this with each other?

The awkwardness is mostly coming from Noah, but Trevor isn't doing anything to help the situation. Luckily, Skyler brings out their food quickly, before it becomes more painfully obvious that Trevor has no idea what to say to Noah right now.

They start eating, and Trevor waits for Noah to start the conversation, but he doesn't seem inclined to bring up whatever it is he wanted to talk about. Trevor and Skyler shoot each other concerned looks as they watch him just sitting there, picking listlessly at his food.

Finally, Skyler jumps in and says, "All right, so what's going on? Because you're kinda freaking us out here. Are you okay?"

Noah visibly cringes before he makes eye contact with Skyler and then Trevor. "I'm sorry. I'm being weird. It's just . . . I have something really big I need to ask of you guys."

Trevor braces himself. "What is it? We're friends, man. You don't have to be so nervous about asking for a favor."

"It's a *really* big favor," Noah reiterates.

Skyler takes a large gulp of his wine, then sets it down a little clumsily, the red liquid almost sloshing out. "Come on. You know we're family. Whatever you need, we've got you."

Trevor smiles at that, because of course it's true. All the guys from the band are family. And they're lucky to have each other. Meeting Skyler was obviously the best thing that came from Trevor reluctantly dragging his nineteen-year-old ass to that audition all those years ago, but growing so close with the rest of the guys was a blessing too.

He's sure not all bands are as close. Especially ones that got put together by a label the way Boys Will Be Boys did. It was almost like fate—how the five of them were each selected separately but came together and bonded so naturally. Or maybe it's just natural to form a bond with people when you're thrown together into a wild, and not exactly healthy, situation. But still, he's grateful for the relationships that came out of all the chaos.

Noah sighs, setting his fork down on the edge of his plate. "Right. So the thing is . . ." He trails off, and Trevor fights the urge to tell him to spit it out already, but then Noah focuses on him. "I know you keep telling me I'm working too much, but I don't exactly have anything going on for me outside of work."

"That can't be true," Skyler interjects.

Noah shrugs uncomfortably. "It is, though. I've got essentially no family, no girl-friend. No hobbies. I asked Trevor for the job because I was burnt out with making my own music and performing. It had stopped being fun for me, and for a while, changing things up felt good. But really, I just swapped one job for another, and now I'm burning myself out on this one too."

Trevor's stomach twists. This is exactly what he was afraid of. He knows he can find someone to replace Noah if he has to. But he enjoys being able to work with his friend. It's hard finding people in this industry you can trust implicitly.

"You can ease up on your workload if you need to," he suggests. "I can pick up more myself or hire someone else, so you can work less hours."

But Noah shakes his head. "I still love being a part of the label. I really do.

And I'm fully aware that I'm the one choosing to work so much. That's not the issue."

"What is it then?" Skyler pries gently.

"I guess my issue is that it's getting harder and harder to escape the reality that my life is kind of pathetic." Running a hand roughly through his hair, Noah adds, "And I know this is no one's problem but my own, but lately I feel like I'm going crazy. Like I want to crawl out of my skin just to get away from myself."

Trevor reaches out, setting his palm on the table between them. "What do you need from us?"

"Well, here comes the big favor," Noah says wryly. "This is going to sound insane, but I need to do *something*. Something I enjoy, something I can be proud of. And the idea that keeps coming back to me is Boys Will Be Boys. I was so damn proud of what we accomplished there, and I want . . . I want to get the band back together."

For a few seconds, no one says anything. Those words have thrown Trevor so far for a loop, he's not sure if he's still sitting in his seat. Is he understanding correctly?

"Not as a permanent thing," Noah goes on. "But maybe for the summer or some-thing. I'm asking if there's any chance you two would be willing to do a reunion tour."

Again, silence.

Trevor looks at Skyler, Skyler looks at him.

Trevor's mind is spinning.

Reunion tours happen all the time. But bands who broke up in such a public, spectacularly disastrous way? Would people even want to give them another chance? And logistically, how they hell could they all make that work? And legally? He'd need to find copies of their old contracts with the label. Because fucking hell, there's no way he wants to make those assholes any extra money if he can help it.

"Is that even possible?" Skyler asks, voicing a summary of all of Trevor's thoughts.

Noah nods. "Yeah, I've looked into it. And I already talked to Oli and Jermaine. They both said they're on board as long as the two of you are."

Trevor narrows his eyes, because this is a lot to throw at him and Skyler, and he's not sure he likes that the other guys were asked separately, when this is obvious-ly a group decision. "Why are you asking us last?"

"Because I know we all went through a lot of bullshit in that band, but I think it was the worst for you guys," Noah explains, picking up his fork just to drag it through his food. "I didn't even want to bring it up with you if Oli and Jermaine were gonna say no. I would've just let it go. I hate that my asking this might be dredging up painful memories."

Yeah, painful is certainly one way to put what Trevor and Skyler went through because of that label and management. Trevor looks over and studies Skyler, trying to gauge his reaction to all this, and ready to reach for him if he's upset. But Skyler's face is hard to read. He doesn't look upset exactly—more like he's still trying to pro-cess this huge request, the same way Trevor is.

And then Skyler says, "Jermaine said yes? It was hard for him, too. In a way the rest of us never had to deal with. All the racism from the label, our management, the media, the public. He should've never been treated like that. I know we did our best to shield him, but we didn't have enough power."

Trevor knows that's something Skyler still regrets, not sticking up for Jermaine more. But they were young, and they did feel powerless in those situations.

Trevor never intends to feel powerless like that again.

Noah sighs heavily as he spears a shrimp on the end of his fork. Then he raises it halfway to his mouth like he's actually going to eat something finally, but he doesn't. "I know. I know how awful it was for him, but most of that originated from the label. They basically set him up to be stereotyped. And we wouldn't be letting them control us or our images anymore, so I think it could be different. Jermaine said he'll do it if everyone else wants to."

"And Oli?" Trevor asks, though it's not as much of a surprise that Oli would be up for this. "He's just going to leave Megan and Emma?"

"Megan said she and Emma would come with us." Setting his fork back down, Noah gets a determined look on his face. "Look, I'm aware that this is too much to ask all of you, but I'm feeling kind of desperate. I would never want to put you through what you went through back then. But we'd do it differently this time, right? It could be like a second chance to do things our way. We'd be doing it for the music and the fans. And for ourselves. I think it could be nice for all of us to do this together one more time, and to do it the right way. Without all the bullshit and pressure. Just the five of us as friends doing something we love."

When Trevor looks to Skyler again, Skyler takes his hand and says, "It does sound kind of cool."

"And I'm sure it would be for the last time," Noah adds. "Because you've all got your own things going on, and I know you guys want to have kids soon. So who knows if we'd ever be able to make this work again in the future."

Skyler squeezes Trevor's hand. "What do you think?"

"I . . ." Jesus, what the hell *does* he think? There are so many thoughts swirling through Trevor's brain right now that he can't even make sense of them. The only thing that makes sense is the feel of his husband's hand in his. So he tells Noah, "I think we need some time to talk about this. Alone. Is that okay if we can't give you an answer tonight?"

"Oh, yeah, of course," Noah says, and now he looks more relieved than he has all night. Even though Trevor didn't give him anything close to a yes. "Obviously, you two should discuss it and take time to consider it. Actually, I can just go and leave you alone now. Thanks for hearing me out."

"Woah, you don't need to leave," Trevor hastens to say.

But Noah is already standing up from the table. "No, really, it's okay. I don't have much of an appetite anyway. Sorry I made you cook for nothing, Sky."

Skyler stands too and grabs Noah's plate. "Hey, you didn't make me do anything. You're our friend, and you are always welcome here for dinner, okay? But why don't I wrap this up for you so you can take it with you?"

After a glance at the food and a moment of hesitation, Noah nods. "Yeah. Thanks."

Trevor abandons his own plate to follow the two of them into the kitchen, where Skyler silently transfers Noah's meal and some extra into a glass container before handing it back to him. Noah looks more than ready to get out of here, so Skyler and Trevor walk him to the door to say goodbye.

As soon as he's gone, Trevor turns to Skyler. For a moment, neither of them speak. Then Skyler lets out an unamused laugh and says, "Well, that was sure unexpected."

"Uh, yeah," Trevor agrees.

With their dinners all but forgotten, they wander into the living room and sit beside each other on the couch. "We can tell him no," Trevor assures Skyler, placing a hand on his husband's leg.

"I know we can," Skyler says. "But we can also say yes, can't we?"

Trevor raises his eyebrows. "You'd really consider doing this? After everything?"

Being in that band almost destroyed Skyler. Almost destroyed them both.

Although Trevor can't blame the label and management for everything. Plenty of the blame for the destruction of Trevor and Skyler's relationship falls on him. He was up against a lot, and not in the best position to fight, but he still should have fought harder.

But he and Skyler agreed to stop worrying about who or what was to blame, didn't they? Because they're together now.

Everything between them is good. It's fucking amazing. And Trevor would never do anything that might risk that.

Skyler shifts closer to him, running his thumb over the tattoo on Trevor's hand. "I remember all the bad shit from before. But I remember all the good parts, too. So much of being in the band together was incredible. And if we figure out a way to bring back all those good times without all the bad . . . if we could all do it one more time together? That sounds kind of perfect."

Trevor looks into Skyler's green eyes and sees the excitement swirling there. He's not totally against the idea. There's just so much to consider. For them, for the rest of the guys. Logistics and legal matters. But if Skyler wants to do this, then they will. There is nothing Trevor wouldn't give Skyler if he has the power to.

Still, he asks, "Are you sure?"

With a smile, Skyler nods. "It'll be like going back to our roots. It sounds fun. And honestly, I think it might be good for me. You know I've been feeling a bit lost this year. Not as lost as Noah, clearly. But being on tour with everyone might inspire me with my own music, help me find a new direction for it. And performing with you is my favorite thing to do."

"It sounds like you've already decided."

"Not without you." Skyler shakes his head violently. "It feels like it might be the right thing for me, but if it's not right for you, then I don't want to do it."

Trevor considers his own feelings, his own life, though it's difficult to separate any part of himself from Skyler. He had the time of his life performing with the band. When it was just about the music and performances, and they could ignore all the rest of the drama. It never felt quite the same when he was doing it on his own for that brief period.

Last year, stepping onto the stage with Skyler each night of his tour to sing "He's Mine" together, watching the crowd sing along, it definitely reminded Trevor how much singing with the love of his life lights him up inside.

It just might be his favorite thing in the world to do, too. After simply *being* with Skyler, of course.

"I think I would love the chance to perform with you again," he realizes. "And the other guys too. But what about our plans for starting a family?"

Skyler gives him the kind of smile that could probably save the world. "You and me are already a family. And we're going to be together for the rest of our lives. We have plenty of time. Like Noah said, we might not all have another chance to do this together. The only thing I'm worried about is your label. I don't want you to have to put everything on hold."

As much as Trevor cares about the label, that didn't even make his list of top concerns. There's no harm in holding off for a while on signing new artists. And he was already planning to hire more staff, so most things could probably stay in motion in his and Noah's absence. A lot of his work is on a computer anyway. He could still run things from the road if he has to.

"I'm not worried about that," he says. "I can make it work if this is something you really want."

"I think it is," Skyler tells him. "Maybe going backward is what I need in order to figure out how I want to move forward."

Trevor laces their fingers together and kisses the back of Skyler's hand. "If this is what you want."

"Is it what *you* want?" Skyler presses him again.

Trevor laughs. "Baby, you know whatever you want is what I want."

Skyler rolls his eyes, but his smile could definitely save the world now. It's that powerful.

And Trevor's power lies in making this man smile.

Their friends will never stop accusing them of being codependent, but he doesn't care. He doesn't care that his happiness is tied to Skyler's, and he's not worried about Skyler's being tied to his. Because Trevor would move a fucking mountain to make Skyler James happy.

He brings Skyler's hand up to his mouth for another kiss, and then he lets it go so that he can hold his baby's face with both hands. After a kiss that makes every molecule in Trevor's body sing a love song, Trevor smiles and says, "So it looks like we're going on tour."

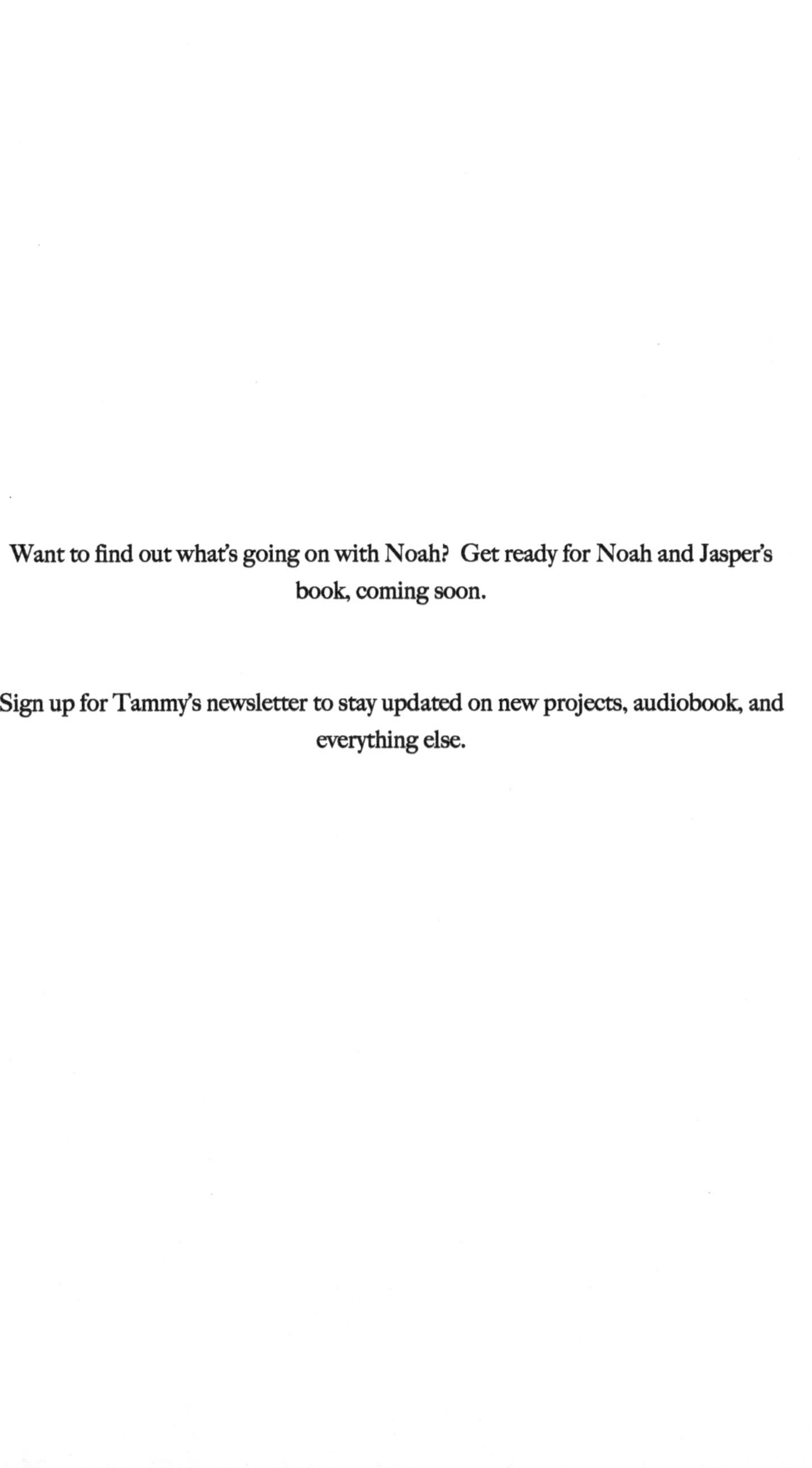

Want to find out what's going on with Noah? Get ready for Noah and Jasper's book, coming soon.

Sign up for Tammy's newsletter to stay updated on new projects, audiobook, and everything else.

ALSO BY THE AUTHOR

HEARTBREAK HONEY

Heartbreak Honey (MM)

Soulmate Symphony (MM)

MAYWEATHER

Maybe We Can Fake It (MM)

STANDALONES

It Always Leads to You (MF)

ABOUT THE AUTHOR

Tammy Subia writes romances that are both sweet and spicy. While most of her stories are M/M, she sometimes spreads the love to other pairings too. If she's not writing or listening to filthy audiobooks, you can find her in New England spoiling her cat, drinking iced matchas, and watching *Gilmore Girls*.

Connect with Tammy: tammysubiabooks

www.ingramcontent.com/pod-product-compliance
Lightning Source LLC
LaVergne TN
LVHW090515110826
845146LV00003B/862

* 9 7 9 8 9 9 1 9 3 6 4 2 2 *